CONTEST OF WILLS

VINCENT H. O'NEIL

W★RLDWIDE®

TORONTO • NEW YORK • LONDON
AMSTERDAM • PARIS • SYDNEY • HAMBURG
STOCKHOLM • ATHENS • TOKYO • MILAN
MADRID • WARSAW • BUDAPEST • AUCKLAND

Recycling programs
for this product may
not exist in your area.

CONTEST OF WILLS

A Worldwide Mystery/August 2012

First published by CreateSpace

ISBN-13: 978-0-373-26810-8

Printed in U.S.A.

Acknowledgments

This book is dedicated to the members of the 10th Mountain Division, United States Army past, present, and future.

Climb to Glory

ONE

"MOST OF THE TIME, what you see doesn't matter. It's what you *don't* see that's important." Jimmy Hanigan said this without looking at me, his eyes roving over a small yellow house just down the block from where we were parked. "You take our guy here, for example. Mr. Dillon. Friday he walks into court pulling an oxygen tank behind him and sucking on the thing like it was filled with milk chocolate. I thought Walter was going to go nuts."

Walter Daley, owner and senior counsel of Daley & Associates law firm in Tallahassee, was our boss. He didn't handle too many cases himself anymore, so I assumed he'd been sitting in the back of the courtroom with Jimmy when all this occurred. My name's Frank Cole, by the way, but you'll hear plenty about me later in the story.

"We'd never seen the guy trundling a SCUBA tank before then, so you know it's a hoax. Probably hoping to play on the jury's sympathies." I knew no such thing, having signed on as Jimmy Hanigan's assistant at Daley & Associates only two months earlier. At first I'd stuck to what I do best, which is internet background checks and retrieval of court documents, but Jimmy believed in on-the-job training. He'd taken me on a wide variety of firm assignments, from depositions to neighborhood door-knocking, and I'd already learned a lot under his tutelage.

I was now sitting behind the wheel of a pickup truck that belonged to one of Jimmy's many friends. He liked to switch vehicles during surveillance jobs like this one, and so we would probably be using this rig only once. I looked away from the yellow house, and was struck once again by the youth of my new mentor in the P.I. business. Jimmy Hanigan was twenty-seven, which made him four years my junior, but he'd been working various jobs in the investigations business for close to ten years.

His hair was jet-black, and his brown eyes were so dark that they might just as well have been black too. He stood a shade under six feet, which made him my height, and his trim physique hid what I already knew was impressive physical strength. I'd seen him pin an uncooperative informant to the wall of an alley one time, and had felt no concern about the struggling man getting away. This morning he was wearing a white collared shirt untucked over a set of blue jeans, and a pair of calf-high black boots that he wore more often than not.

"But hoax or no, the jury saw it, and so now we have to prove Mr. Dillon's playing a game. Like I said, most of the time it's not what you see that helps you discredit something like this—it's what you don't see. I made some calls over the weekend, and I learned that anybody working that hard on that size oxygen tank is going to have to get it refilled within a couple of days."

"So we're going to sit here until we see him take the thing for a fill-up?" I'd been employed on the periphery of the P.I. business for over a year by then, and had developed the habit of questioning much of what was said to me. Off the top of my head I could see three or four ways we could be thwarted in this quest. Additionally, I'd once sat with Jimmy in the back of a small van for an entire day and night, and didn't really want to try it again.

"That's not what I'm saying." His forehead wrinkled momentarily, but he still didn't look at me. I thought for a moment that the rising Florida sun had caused him to squint like that, but then saw that he'd simply found my question silly. "That was just one example. Here's another: someone with a breathing problem like that should be receiving regular medical attention. So if we don't see him go to a clinic, or get a visit from some home health-care outfit, it all helps us prove his little breathing apparatus is a prop."

"And exactly what does that do in court?" Jimmy knew a lot about the law, and more than once I'd found him discussing nuanced legal points with Walter.

"It's not so much a court thing, actually. If we can gather enough evidence that Mr. Dillon's a fake, Walter will let the other side know we can make their guy look like a fool. They'll have to respond to that, because our next step *will* be in court. We'll wait until Mr. Dillon's on the stand, ask him who his doctor is, how often he visits, that kind of thing. Once the answers are on record, we'll shoot them down one by one.

"After that it can get really embarrassing for the other

side, particularly if it's a no-nonsense judge." He finally looked at me, but only for an instant. "Walter's on very good terms with a lot of the robes in the Panhandle, so the other side can expect real trouble if Walter dimes them."

I was about to ask how long we were expected to watch Mr. Dillon when something caused Jimmy to lean closer to the windshield. I looked down the street again, and then glanced at the photo sitting between us on the truck's bench seat. Jimmy had snapped that picture at the end of court the previous week, and I now recognized Mr. Dillon as he came out his front door.

It was a quiet neighborhood, but Monday was getting started and so there were people out and about. Some were going to work, some were walking dogs, and a couple, like our friend from the oxygen-tank story, seemed to be getting ready to go for a jog. The Mr. Dillon before us was a thin middle-aged man, dressed in running shorts and a sweatshirt, and we watched in silent amazement as he went through a long series of stretching exercises. No oxygen bottle, or assistance of any other kind, was in sight.

I spoke slowly, as if stupid. "So you were saying we wouldn't actually *see* what we needed, and that it was what we *didn't* see—" I never finished that barb, as Jimmy began hissing orders over his shoulder while searching the truck's floor for the appropriate tools.

"We need to get shots of this." He handed me a camera, knowing that I'd been trained in its use by my girlfriend, a photography instructor at a local community college. "Scrunch down and rest the lens on the side mirror so he doesn't see what you're doing. Try not to zoom in too much. We need to show he's outside his house."

Both of the truck's windows were open in the early-morning heat, and I soon had a nice shot of Mr. Dillon doing an impressive side stretch right in front of his doorstep. The camera was digital, and I confirmed that I had captured the moment just as Hanigan came up with a camcorder and the day's newspaper.

"Okay, here's what we'll do. He'll run off in a bit, and we'll follow him nice and slow. There's a park near here, popular place for the runners, and if we're lucky he'll do a few laps."

WE STAYED WELL BACK, which was easy because Mr. Dillon took off at a very respectable clip. Jimmy got some footage of him speeding down the street until, as predicted, he hopped onto the running trail at a local park. The path went around a small pond before being obscured for a distance by some trees, and close to a dozen people were already jogging in the new morning's sun.

Jimmy directed me to a parking space with a good vantage point, and we let Mr. Dillon go by once so that we could select the proper public bench. I held the camcorder low in the window, panning it left and right to show our surroundings while waiting for our quarry to return. I had to admire Mr. Dillon's grace when he came back around and passed a man seated on one of the park's benches. The man had one black boot crossed over the other, and his face was obscured by the front page of the local paper.

"Well that was quick, I'll say that," Jimmy commented as he hopped back in and took the camera from me. He watched the replay, nodding his head in approval, and then handed it back. I looked into the viewer, and soon saw Mr. Dillon running past a very legible shot of that day's paper.

"Went jogging three days after appearing in court wheeling an oh-two tank." I looked over at Jimmy. "Not very smart, is he?"

"Most of 'em aren't. I've seen disability frauds working secret jobs, shot footage of guys with supposedly bad backs tossing cinder blocks into dump trucks." Hanigan took the camcorder from me and began seating it in its case. "You gotta love the dumb ones, though. They give us more time to work on the smart ones."

WE DECIDED TO SHOOT a little more film of Mr. Dillon as he jogged home, and then Hanigan said we should head for the barn.

That was his little way of saying we were going back to the law office, but it was by no means a surprising turn of phrase. Hanigan had been raised in nearby Tallahassee, but he could switch from a full-on Southern accent to an unidentifiable monotone in the middle of a sentence. He could do the same thing mentally, too, sounding like a college professor one moment and then coming across as a country bumpkin the next. His ability to adapt to just about any given situation came in

handy when we were going door-to-door, but I sometimes wondered if I knew the real Jimmy Hanigan at all.

We grabbed a celebratory breakfast on the way, and
pulled into the parking lot of Daley & Associates around
midmorning. A waist-high hedge ran around the white
building, which looked more like a large private home
than a law office. It fit well with the surrounding neighborhood, which consisted of middle-class houses and
fenced-in backyards. It was early fall in the Panhandle,
which meant it was rapidly getting hot outside.

We went up a cement walkway to a black-painted
front door that sported a large brass knocker. The
knocker was circular, and its base was formed by two
hands holding a heart wearing a crown. Walter Daley
was proud of his Irish ancestry, and the hands-and-
crowned-heart symbol was known as the Claddagh
among the children of the Emerald Isle. I had found it
a welcoming symbol long before Walter told me that
was one of its meanings.

We passed inside, entering a large reception area
bustling with the new day's activity. The interior of
Daley & Associates was painted in light colors, with
an emphasis on white, yellow and tan. The floors were
hardwood and covered with rugs, potted plants guarded
the walls, and the whole effect left me wondering if I'd
walked into a law office or some rich man's club.

The clothing gave it away, however, as Jimmy and I
were the only ones in casual dress. Lawyers and para-
legals wearing business suits could be seen in the long
main hallway behind the foyer, and we exchanged good-

mornings with two of the receptionists as we passed
on through.

Hanigan was not on good terms with some of the
more senior lawyers in the building, and I had not yet
summoned the nerve to ask why. He usually made a
point of ignoring them, and I assumed he was simply
making it clear that he answered to one boss, Walter.
The flip side of that dynamic was interesting, though;
Hanigan seemed on excellent terms with every novice,
paralegal and gopher in the place.

He was also friendly with Emil Tabor, the office
manager, and I considered this to be a major point in
his favor. I'd had a crackerjack office manager in the
company I'd briefly owned in another life, and believed
that only a fool would alienate the individual who keeps
the whole place running. We passed Emil in the long,
white-paneled corridor, which led to Walter's office,
but Tabor was busy upbraiding one of the firm's star
litigators and didn't seem to notice us.

"I don't care how many cases you've won this year,
Bernie—although I do know it isn't as many as you've
been saying. My staff has to be able to program its
workload, and you can't bring your notes to the typists
at three in the afternoon and expect them to be ready
the next day."

"Listen, Emil, I'm not going to argue with you about
this." Bernie Kaplan was the fastest horse in Walter's
stable, but he had an ego that rankled much of the staff.
I looked back briefly to see the chubby, dark-haired
attorney wagging a finger at the thin, unconcerned

office manager, and wondered what made Bernie think he stood a snowball's chance of winning the argument.

Hanigan knocked on Walter Daley's door even though it stood open. Walter's office occupied a back corner of the building's ground floor, and its main feature was a wall of large windows. These looked out on the picnic area out back which many Daley & Associates employees used for their lunch breaks. A big part of Walter's self-image rested in his ability to provide for others, and the lunch area was just one more indication of his role as father figure and tribal chieftain.

"Jimmy. Frank. Come on in." Walter was seated behind an enormous carved desk, and he finished reading a typed page of something while we took seats in front of him. His office was a cross between a study and a Gaelic museum, as the walls were covered with the Daley family's coat of arms, maps of Ireland from Roman times to the modern era, and paintings of Irish farmers and fishermen plying their trades. The rugs on the floor looked like medieval tapestries, and the room's white walls were interrupted at regular intervals by rich brown paneling.

Daley put the paper down and settled back in his chair. He was a short man, but his shoulders were impressively broad. He almost always wore a vested suit to work, and the wheat-colored fabric of that day's outfit wrapped around his barrel chest like armor. His dark hair was shot through with gray, but his face showed very few wrinkles.

"You'll like this one," Jimmy began, and Walter smiled expectantly. The lilt of Irish laughter was never far from our employer's light blue eyes, and Hanigan seemed to have a knack for entertaining him. "Mr. Dillon went jogging this morning, without his oxygen tank, and Frank caught it all on tape. I looked it over, and it's all you'll need if you want to make an issue of this."

Walter's lips pressed against each other as if he were trying not to laugh, and he shook his head in disbelief. "What an idiot. It was crazy of him to bring that thing into court to begin with, but he must be ten different kinds of stupid to then go and pull a stunt like this."

"That's what we said."

"I can imagine." Walter shook his head once or twice more, and then leaned forward to put his arms on the desk. The sleeves of his white shirt were rolled almost to his elbows, forming creaseless strips which rested in exactly the same spot on both forearms. "Listen. We've got a new one, and I want you to drop everything else until you've got this taken care of."

I pulled out a small notebook and pencil while Jimmy slid forward on his chair. I'd never heard Walter start an assignment that way before, and I guessed Jimmy hadn't either.

"We drew up a will for an ailing client a couple of months ago, and unfortunately he died last week. He had a heart attack in his sleep, but the will was in his possession and is now missing—" Hanigan gave a small whistle at this "—so we need to find out what happened to it. Hopefully it's just misplaced, but if it can't be found the estate is going to be divided in a fashion that is not in accordance with our client's wishes."

Jimmy looked at me and spoke. "Under Florida law,

if the will can't be found, the assumption is that the testator destroyed it, with the intention of invalidating it."

"Testator?" I asked, never ceasing to be amazed at Jimmy Hanigan's legal repertoire.

"The individual making out the will. So if this will is gone, the estate is divvied up as if the dead man hadn't made a will at all."

"That's right." Walter nodded approvingly at his lead investigator before turning to me. "The dead man in question was a very wealthy local named Chester Pratt. He was a widower up until two years ago, when he remarried. He has a daughter and a son from the previous marriage, and he'd left the bulk of his money to the daughter in the will prepared by this office."

"Isn't that unusual? What's his wife expected to live on?" I posed this question while scribbling madly.

"The second wife and the son were well taken care of in the missing will. The wife got the house, everything in it, and roughly a million dollars. The son got just under a million. Furthermore, the daughter has been administering Chet Pratt's charitable giving for years. She's the business brains in the family now that Chet is gone.

"At the time we created the will, Chet wanted to put his daughter in the driver's seat. His estate is currently valued at roughly forty million dollars, so he felt he was positioning her to continue running the charity, and also to help out the second wife or the son as she saw fit.

"Unfortunately, that's not the way the estate is cut up if the will can't be found. In that case the second wife gets roughly half, and the two children split the rest.

Not exactly what Chet Pratt had in mind when he told
me his last wishes."

I stopped writing for a moment. "Aren't there copies
of the will somewhere?"

"Sure. We've got copies of our own, but under most
circumstances they can't be submitted in probate. It's
the original, or nothing."

"You said this will was only two months old. The
man dies in his sleep, and then his new will goes missing. That sounds a little suspicious." Hanigan had a fine
feel for the dark side of things.

"That's what the police think. The autopsy proved
it was a heart attack, but the blood tests haven't come
back yet. Right now they believe he died from a prescription drug interaction."

That one got by me, and even Hanigan screwed up
his face for a moment before asking the big question.
"But if they don't have the test results, what makes them
suspect something that specific?"

"This is where it gets a little confusing. Chet had a
close call a year and a half ago. He wasn't a well man,
and so he was taking medication for his heart and a couple of other things. The drugs interacted unexpectedly,
and he had a mild attack. They saved him at the hospital, and so of course they changed his drug regimen.
He was still taking the same heart pills, but they took
him off the other medication that caused his close call.

"The night he died he was reading in his study late at
night, after his wife had gone to bed. It seems he nodded off down there, and then had the heart attack that
killed him. Belinda—his second wife—found him in

the morning. She tried her best to revive him, but he was already gone.

"When the daughter, Kerry, called me with the bad news I told her to get control of the will. It was kept in Chet's safe, but when she looked it wasn't there. So they started searching the study. That's when they found a baggy containing some of the old medication, the pills that almost killed him, in his desk drawer."

Walter took a breath before continuing. "Nothing's certain, but it seems that Chet kept some of those pills when Belinda thought she'd thrown them all away. His quality of life wasn't anything to write home about, and it's possible that he killed himself. That's why the police think they already know what the toxicology report will say."

The three of us let that one sit for a while, mostly because it so clearly affected Walter. It was hard to tell if he and Pratt had been close friends, but Walter had a habit of emotionally adopting people and frequently extended that to clients.

"So you'd like us to see if we can locate the will," Jimmy offered after a time.

"That, or at least come up with a time frame for when it vanished. Try to determine when it was last seen. Who knows? Maybe he did destroy the thing. He originally wanted Belinda to get his entire estate, but she wanted most of it to go to the kids. She made him get the new will, basically to keep from being called a gold digger, but I don't think Chet was happy about it.

"He was like that—a little headstrong. Initially Belinda wanted to sign a prenup, but Chet wouldn't hear of it. We drew up a will for him when they first got married, leaving her most of his estate, but apparently he didn't tell her about it at the time. When she found out, she made him get the new one." Walter shook his head. "At any rate, I'd like you to try to fill in some of the blanks here. Find out if the will was always kept in the safe, who had access to it, and if anybody can recall Chet making any comments about going back on the thing.

"Belinda is as interested in resolving this as I am, so she's waiting for you at their house. The daughter, Kerry Pratt-Graham, will be there, too. Be tactful, but get the answers."

We both rose to leave, but I stopped at the door. "Walter?"

"Yes, Frank?"

"Who's the client on this one? We're talking to the widow and the daughter, and probably the son later on. Who's the client?"

"Chester Pratt, Frank. The man who told us how he wanted his estate divided after his death. That's our client."

TWO

WE STOPPED BY Emil's office on the way out. I'd been working at Daley & Associates long enough to know that the office manager would be holding the background materials we would need, as well as the answers to any additional questions.

"Here you are, Jimmy," Emil said, meeting us at the door and handing a colored file to Hanigan. "That poor man was in here not three months ago, getting his will made up."

Emil's hair was a sandy-brown, and he looked genuinely affronted by the Pratt case. That wasn't surprising; he ran a very tight ship and there wasn't a single scrap of paper in that office that he couldn't lay his hands on in five minutes. Emil had been a paralegal for a number of years before Walter elevated him to office manager, and so he was conversant in everything the firm handled.

"How'd he look to you? Health-wise, I mean." Hanigan asked this while quickly scanning the top sheet inside the file.

"It was clear he was not a well man, but I was surprised to hear that he'd died all the same. He was pleasant to talk to, obviously intelligent, and the staff members who took his information say he listed his assets from memory."

"Pleasant, huh? He seem like anything was bothering him?" Jimmy's questions might sound out of place in a discussion with the office majordomo, if you didn't know that Emil could size up a total stranger from a block away.

"This was not a happy occasion for Mr. Pratt or his wife. He had intended to leave his entire estate to Mrs. Pratt, but she apparently felt the bulk of the money should go to the children from the first marriage. He decided to give the daughter most of the estate, and believed that was probably going to cause some friction with the son." Walter and Emil spent a lot of time together, and kept each other informed about the firm's business.

"Thanks, Emil." Jimmy started walking toward the door, still looking at the contents of the file. I followed him, wondering why he hadn't asked Emil's opinion of the wife, Belinda.

I didn't get to think about that for long, though, as Hanigan gave me the file and told me to read it while he drove. It was just as well that Jimmy was driving, as I actually live in a small town on the Florida coast and still did not know Tallahassee all that well. I quickly saw that we were headed back to Hanigan's apartment, and decided that my mentor felt we needed to get into some more respectable clothes.

My adopted town of Exile is a little too far away for me to commute, so I found myself sleeping on Hanigan's sofa at least once a week. We kept some very odd hours in that job, and so I'd moved some clothes into one of Hanigan's closets. It was slightly reminiscent of the early days of my now-defunct software company up north, when I'd spent so much time at work that I sometimes slept in my office.

"It says here that Pratt met with Walter about a possible prenuptial agreement a couple of years ago." The folder contained the background information on the firm's business with Chester Pratt, and would be left in the truck when we got to the Pratt residence.

"Not surprising, considering the man's health and how much money was at stake."

"But it goes on to say that Pratt was only asking in terms of how a will could thwart a prenup." I paused, trying to remember. "Walter did say it was the second wife—Belinda—who wanted the agreement, and that Pratt was against it."

"Hmm." That came out as little more than a grunt. "That is a little odd. You'd think the one with the money would want that protection. I wonder why the old man was against it."

"Both Walter and Emil said Pratt wanted to leave the estate to his wife, so maybe he thought it wasn't worth the effort."

"Maybe. We'll have to see if we can find a delicate way to ask that one." We pulled into the apartment complex that Hanigan called home, and rolled around an interior driveway bordered by well-kept palm trees. The buildings were long two-story affairs, with open-air stairwells and breezeways which cut straight through the structure. The clientele was mostly young professionals, and we passed a pool and fitness center along the way.

Jimmy parked outside his place and killed the engine. "Listen, Frank. We need to be very careful with the way we talk to the family. The old man's dead, there's a lot of money up for grabs, and the will's missing. We have no idea who hates who here, so the potential for finger-pointing is huge. We need to help find that will if it still exists, and get a good idea of when it was last seen if it's been destroyed. That's it."

His coaching reminded me of our conversation with Walter, where Jimmy had displayed his usual familiarity with the legal workings of Daley & Associates. I decided this was a good opportunity to ask the question that had been bothering me for weeks.

"Jim, just how is it that you know so much law?"

I half expected him to tell me that he'd soaked it up through osmosis, after having spent so much time with the firm's lawyers and their clients, but as usual he surprised me. Hopping out of the truck on his side, he brought a finger to his lips and gave me a playful shake of the head before shutting the door with a thud.

THE PRATT RESIDENCE was somewhat smaller than I expected. I was once married to a girl from an obscenely wealthy family, and so I associated money like the Pratts' with tennis courts, stone walls and security gates. The Pratt house sat on a quiet cul-de-sac shaped like a lollipop, and although it was obviously an affluent community the houses around them were not mansions.

The place where we pulled up was a brown two-story house with a porch running along the front and one side. A grassy yard sloped down to the street, and two overflowing flower beds suggested someone inside had quite a green thumb. Planters hung from the porch roof, and their tendrils reached down toward a pair of rattan chairs and a swing near the front door.

We parked on the street because the driveway already held a blue BMW sports car and a maroon Mercedes sedan. Looking around while donning the lightest sports coat I owned, I noted another Mercedes parked at a neighbor's house across the circle. The circle itself sported a stone sun dial and even more flowers, and I decided that the place looked rich enough without the mansions.

Jimmy walked ahead of me up a short brick walkway, still wearing the boots under a pair of khaki trousers, a blue blazer and a red tie. It had been over a week since the death of Mr. Pratt, but we were going to be walking on eggshells here and it was important to make a good impression.

THE FRONT DOOR OPENED before we got there, and a middle-aged woman with blond hair stepped out onto the porch. She was followed by a younger woman with brown hair, and I guessed that we were looking at Pratt's widow and his daughter.

"Hello. Walter said to expect you. I'm Belinda Pratt, and this is my stepdaughter, Kerry." She was a big woman, only slightly overweight even though I could now see that she was in late middle age. Though aware of our visit's purpose, Belinda Pratt was the picture of Southern hospitality. She wore a dark gray dress with a black belt, and did her best to smile as Jimmy took her hand in both of his.

"Please accept my deepest sympathies, Mrs. Pratt," Jimmy began, the Southern accent making a slight reappearance. "I'm Jim Hanigan, and this is my partner Frank Cole. I do hope we haven't come at an inconvenient time."

Mrs. Pratt exhaled softly. "I'm afraid I'm not thinking in terms of convenient and inconvenient right now, Mr. Hanigan. It's been a difficult time here, as you can imagine."

"I understand." I'd seen Hanigan's gift for morphing into different personalities many times before, but this time I felt his empathy was genuine. "Walter thought we might be able to help."

He disengaged his right hand and extended it toward Pratt's daughter, who was standing in the doorway. I would have guessed her age at late thirties, and she looked like she got to the gym more than once a week. Her face was pleasant-looking without being pretty, and her brown eyes suggested a probing intelligence. She wore a beige business suit, and dark brown hair hung almost down to her shoulders. "It's Mrs. Graham, isn't it?"

"Pratt-Graham, actually. I kept my father's name." Her voice was only a little louder than Belinda's. "Thank you for coming."

Hanigan turned back to the widow. "We won't take up any more of your time than is absolutely necessary, Mrs. Pratt. Is there somewhere we could sit and talk?"

Belinda led us inside, and we passed through a

furniture-packed living room and a short hallway before entering some kind of study. Compared to the show-houses owned by my former in-laws, the Pratt residence was impressively lived-in. Many of my ex-wife's friends and relatives had owned houses that looked like something in a magazine, and so the sight of a book carelessly tossed on a side table, or a hall rug with a corner turned under, was a welcome change.

Pratt's study took this image a little too far, though. The center of the room's gold carpet was taken up by tall stacks of hardcover books. These had been removed from the now-empty shelves of the study's back wall, which stood out from the brown molding in large expanses of beige. A smaller pile of manila folders, business envelopes and boxes of things too small to stack together sat right next to the books. I guessed this detritus had come from the desk, a large piece of expensive furniture that sat catty-cornered near the bookcases. Not surprisingly, someone had been giving the place a thorough search.

"I suppose I don't have to ask if you've looked for the will," Jimmy commented breezily, opening a palm toward the books and smiling just a little at Belinda.

"We've been over every inch of this room, Mr. Hanigan," Mrs. Pratt answered, looking and sounding like someone approaching her wit's end. "And we haven't found anything. Except, of course…"

She wasn't able to finish, so her stepdaughter came up and put an arm around her. She didn't start sobbing or anything, but I guessed she was reliving the discovery of the pills in Mr. Pratt's desk.

As an excuse to look elsewhere, I surveyed the rest of the room. Two windows looked out on a large wooden deck which descended to an inground swimming pool, and I could see child-size swim fins and goggles hanging on its fence. Near the windows sat a well-used reading chair and a tall floor lamp. A man-size globe that was way out of date stood in the far corner, and several framed reproductions of old maps hung on the wall near the bookcases. Looking behind the desk, I saw a floor-level wall safe whose door stood wide open.

A step closer showed me the inside was empty, but it was clear from the door's thickness that the box was fireproof. I motioned toward it with my head after catching Hanigan's eye, and he walked over to have a look.

Mrs. Pratt had composed herself by then, but her stepdaughter took over the conversation. "Yes, that's my father's safe. The will was kept in there, along with these other items—" she indicated a box next to the desk, in which I could see several old photo albums and yellowing envelopes of various sizes "—and for the life of me I can't imagine him putting the will anywhere else."

Jimmy nodded, still the picture of sympathy. "Is there any way for us to determine the last time the will was seen?"

"Actually, yes. We celebrated my father's birthday here the night of his heart attack, and Belinda had made up a special present for him using some of his older photographs." She pointed at the box again, the one holding the contents of the safe.

"It was a collage of reprints, pictures of his family

when he was a little boy." Mrs. Pratt had regained her voice, but the topic sounded like it would set her to crying again shortly. "I sneaked the albums out without him noticing, and the people at the store were so helpful…anyway, when I put them back I saw the folder that held the will."

"Was that a Daley & Associates folder?" Jimmy asked.

"Yes. It was cream-colored, with Walter's emblem." The heart-and-hands Claddagh symbol adorned just about everything produced by the firm. "You couldn't miss it."

"I see. So when was that?"

"Three days before the party. I had the pictures scanned, and returned the albums as soon as I could."

"So your husband went into the safe frequently?"

"I wouldn't call it frequent, but he kept important things in there. He probably opened it at least once a week."

"Excuse me for asking this, but who had the combination?"

"My husband, of course, and me, and Kerry." Pratt's widow noticed what she'd said just then, and added, "Kerry worked very closely with her father, managing his charity work. All of his papers were in that safe."

Pratt's daughter stepped up to that one. "I called your boss as soon as we got back from the hospital that morning. He said I should take control of the will, so I went into the safe. It wasn't there when I looked."

"You mean the folder was empty, or the folder was gone, as well?"

"There was no folder, and no will, when I checked." Kerry reached into one of the nearby book boxes and removed a cream-colored, hard-backed Daley & Associates document cover. "We did find this stuck in the bookcase when we were searching, but there was nothing in it."

Jimmy took the case and popped the button snap which held it shut. It had two inside document flaps, and a clear plastic pocket for a business card. All three were empty.

"Do you think this was the file that contained the will?"

"It might be." Belinda spoke up. "Chester had two wills drawn up by Walter, one when we were newly married and then the most recent one."

"Walter mentioned that. I believe the first one left the bulk of the estate to you, Mrs. Pratt?"

"Yes. Chet had that drawn up without my knowledge, but when I found out about it I made him change it."

"Mrs. Pratt, are you sure you saw a Daley & Associates folder in the safe just before the party? It's important."

"Yes, I am. I saw it when I first took the pictures out, and I saw it when I put them back."

"The will was the newest thing in the safe, Mr. Hanigan," Kerry added. "It sat right on top. I saw it myself several times."

Jimmy nodded. "I see. Can you tell me, roughly, what time you found the folder missing?"

"It would have been ten o'clock in the morning, maybe ten-thirty. We were a long time at the hospital."

"I'm assuming that no one was here while you were gone? At the hospital, I mean."

"No," Mrs. Pratt answered. "I called Belinda when the ambulance got here, and she and Neil came right over. The three of us went to the hospital then."

"I'm sorry. Neil is...who?"

Kerry fielded that one. "My husband. Neil Graham."

"Who else did you call?"

"No one. We decided to wait before calling my brother. He didn't handle my father's earlier attack very well, and we even discussed not telling him the bad news over the phone. But we finally decided to call him from the hospital, and he and his wife came down as soon as they got someone to watch their youngest."

"Does anyone else have access to the house? A cleaning service, for example?"

Kerry turned to Belinda, who answered, "We have a service, but only members of the family have keys. Kerry has one and Thomas has one, but that's it."

I'd been taking this all down in my notebook while trying to stand off to the side, and Jimmy gave me a look asking if I was caught up. I nodded back, and he continued.

"Just a few more questions, Mrs. Pratt, and we'll be going. You said there was a birthday party here that night?"

"Yes." Belinda looked ready to crumble right then and there, which explained why Hanigan had held that part to the end. "Chester's. I'm sure Walter told you that my husband's plans for his estate had caused some bad feelings in the family, but I remember thinking at the party that everyone was getting along so well, that maybe the whole thing was finally settled. And now this."

She looked away, and Kerry stepped up yet again. "It was just a family affair. My father, Belinda, me and my husband, and my brother and his family."

"No outsiders?"

"No."

"When did that take place?"

"Roughly from six to nine." Kerry looked at Belinda, who nodded in agreement. Jimmy placed a hand on the widow's arm, and I knew the interview was over.

"Again, I am so sorry for your loss. We're very concerned about locating the will, and so we're going to need to speak with everyone who was in the house from the time you last saw the will to when it was discovered missing. Can you help us with that?"

"Of course. It's what Chester would have wanted."

"What happens if the will isn't found?" Kerry asked quietly.

"Walter will do his best to get an exception, and have a copy of the will accepted into probate, but that's probably not going to work." Hanigan was speaking to both of the women up until then, but I saw that he was watching Kerry closely when he added, "But you knew that already."

"Yes," Kerry answered with a regretful nodding, her lips pressing together afterward. If Jimmy had expected a guilty reaction from her, he didn't get it. I was familiar with that little trick, the sentence that sounds normal to everyone except someone who has something to hide. Either Kerry was also familiar with it, or she didn't see what Hanigan was doing.

I didn't get to ask Jimmy if that was what he'd been doing, or even why we hadn't offered to help look for the will. We said our goodbyes, and he tossed me the keys once we were in the driveway. He didn't speak for a bit, simply sitting there with a pensive look as I drove us away. After a few blocks I decided he'd had enough time to get his thoughts together.

"You think somebody took the will once the old man was pronounced dead?"

"I hope so."

"You hope so?"

"Yeah. Because if it was taken beforehand, it means someone knew he was going to die."

"Think it was somebody who was unhappy with the way things were going to be handed out?"

"Yep. And everybody who stood to gain or lose from that will…was at that man's birthday party."

THREE

"NOT EXACTLY," Walter contradicted Jimmy almost as soon as we'd finished telling him about our trip. "Sure, everybody at the party was in the will, but that wasn't everyone who had an interest in Chet's estate. Remember he was giving away a lot of money to charities, but none of that was carved in stone. Kerry could have decided to change who was getting that money, or stopped donating altogether if she inherited the bulk of the estate."

"Are you saying that the local library sent someone out to break into Pratt's safe and steal his will?" Hanigan was showing yet another of his many unusual skills, sounding deferential while asking Walter if he were crazy.

"Of course not. I'm saying we can't limit the list of people who might be involved here just because there was a party at Chet's house the night he died. We can't afford to make any assumptions at this point, about anything. We won't even know what caused his heart attack until the toxicology report comes back, and maybe not even then.

"If that shows what we expect, then we'll know the same drug interaction he experienced a while back was the cause of death. But regardless of what was found in his desk, it won't prove he died by his own hand. There is an awful lot of money at stake here, and we can't rule anything out. Or anybody."

"I thought we were just trying to see if we could find the will, or at least establish when it was last seen." I pointed that out in a low voice, and not just because I was new to these discussions. It had sounded like a lazy approach when we'd first been given this assignment, and now I was honestly intrigued by some of the things we'd learned so far. So it had to be said.

"That's right, Frank, but I think you already accomplished that. You say Belinda saw the will three days before the party, which leaves three days for it to be removed before Chet died. It also leaves a few hours after he died, for anybody who knew what had happened."

"Only three people knew the combination to the safe," Jimmy murmured. "Pratt, his wife, and his daughter. Those same people had keys to the house. And all three of them were at the hospital at the same time."

"So it's more likely that the thing was missing beforehand." Walter gave this a moment before continuing. "Before we start guessing here, let's get some more facts together. Jimmy, contact your friends in the police and find out where they are with the investigation. I know it's early, but they're probably leaning one way or the other.

"Frank, I'll call ahead and arrange for you to go back out to the Pratt house and speak to Kerry again. I'll have her assemble a list of the major recipients of Chet's donations, and I want you to review that list with her. Find out just how much contact these people had with Chet, and see if anybody was worried about the charity's future.

"Then I want you to do what you do best, and check their backgrounds. For the most part, Chet's donations went to organizations instead of individuals, so this won't be as hard as it sounds. We're looking for red flags here, things like people accusing the recipient organizations of misusing funds. Be on watch for anything that might suggest an overdependence on Chet's generosity."

"Walter." Hanigan spoke with his eyes on the floor. "No stranger did this. The whole family was in the house hours before the old man died. The only question is if the will was removed after the heart attack... or before."

"I know that." It was Walter's turn to look down now, but he didn't do it for long. "But we have to be thorough. We start with a wide circle, and slowly constrict it. Regardless of how Chet died, or when the will disappeared, our client's wishes are being circumvented. And I'm not going to allow that."

It sounded like Hanigan and I had just been assigned a murder investigation by the dead man's lawyer, so I had to ask. "Walter, exactly what are we trying to do here? Get somebody to confess to taking the will?"

"You hit it on the head. I don't believe Chet would draw up a will and then destroy it without telling me. If I'm right, that means someone else took the thing and probably got rid of it. Without the original, there's almost no way we can get Chet's last wishes enforced." He fixed those blue eyes on me. "There is a provision of the law, however, which says that if we can show that the will fell into the hands of someone who stood to gain by its destruction, we might be allowed to submit the copy of the will that we have on record. But that's a very tough process, and I'd say we're going to need a confession to make it work.

"Find out what happened here, boys. Find out who did this. And make them say it."

I STAYED AT THE FIRM for a few more hours, mining the various online databases which were my stock in trade. Being an assistant in-house investigator was a good gig in a lot of ways, not the least of which was the top-notch equipment and access to a lot of pay-to-use systems on the Net. It didn't take me long to get the basic backgrounds on the beneficiaries in Chester Pratt's missing will, or to notice that they didn't look like any rich family I'd ever known.

I already mentioned that the Pratt house was much smaller than they could afford, but I'd just chalked that up to the old saw about rich people getting rich by pinching their pennies until they screamed. What struck me about the Pratt family, though, was that they all worked full-time and none of them seemed desperate to get at Mr. Pratt's millions.

His widow, Belinda, had come into the family late in life, and I found her name on the retirement roles of a major southeastern bank chain where she'd worked as a statistician. Kerry Pratt-Graham, his daughter, was a licensed investment advisor who was good enough at her job to speak at a large number of financial services conventions (which explained why the old man had tapped her to run his charity).

If the family had an underachiever it was Thomas, the son, but even he wasn't sitting around waiting for better days. He'd run two restaurants into the ground before getting the formula right, and was listed in several papers as the owner-operator of a moderately successful upscale eatery in Tallahassee.

Kerry Graham's husband, Neil, was a financial advisor like his wife, but he had his own business and appeared to be doing very well with it. Thomas's wife, Lindsay, didn't appear to have a job, but the three kids she had with Thomas probably took up most of her energies.

Maybe I was relying too much on the bad example set by my ex-in-laws, but I'd expected to find a group of layabouts in the Pratt family. As near as I could tell from my research, they were a hard-working bunch with no criminal records of any kind, not even when Kerry and Thomas had been of an age to be sowing wild oats. Very few of my former relatives could make such a claim.

Still, nothing I'd seen or learned fit the puzzle posed by the missing will. Belinda Pratt and her stepdaughter, Kerry, had struck me as a pair of open, decent ladies trying to deal with the loss of a husband and father. And yet someone with access to the Pratt house, someone who probably knew the safe's combination, had taken the old man's will. Belinda and Kerry were the only people, other than Chester himself, who knew the combination to the safe. They also had keys to the house.

There are ways to get past a locked door, and to open a safe without the combination, but it didn't help that the two open and decent ladies had access to both places. One said she'd seen the will prior to the party, and the other had gone looking for it the next day. If Belinda had indeed seen Pratt's will in the safe three days before the birthday celebration, then whoever took the document did so shortly before or directly after the man's death.

If the theft of the will was a spur-of-the-moment thing, then the culprit would have already had access to the house and the safe. That pointed the finger of suspicion at Belinda or Kerry, and made me a rotten judge of character.

No matter what it said about me, I did hope that one of the ladies had panicked after returning from the hospital and simply lifted the will. If that were the case, the document could still be in existence and might even turn up somewhere.

If that were not the case, and the theft of the will had been planned, then things got much more serious. That would create a number of additional suspects, people who didn't necessarily need a key to the house or the combination to the safe. It also meant there was a good chance that someone had murdered Chester Pratt.

"FRANK, YOU ARE just awful. Suspecting total strangers just because they're named in a will," Beth Ann Thibedault scolded me as we sped down the highway. She taught a night class in photography at Farragut Community College, and on those evenings I was usually able to run down there and scoop her up for a late dinner.

"A *missing* will," I pointed out, taking the appropriate exit for Beth Ann's place. My own digs in the seaside community of Exile were just too far from Tallahassee for me to make that trip during the week, and I sometimes was allowed to remain at Beth Ann's when we stayed out too late. I spent those nights on the couch, but still it was a good sign that our relationship, strained over the summer by my lack of steady employment, had improved.

I'd moved to Exile from New England more than a year before, just after the software firm that I'd built from scratch had finally gone belly up. All my money had gone into that business, and when it died it had taken my marriage, as well. As if that weren't bad enough, a bankruptcy judge who disliked me had attached my future earnings to pay off the venture (vulture) capitalists who had ruined me.

My old college roommate, a New York lawyer named Mark Ruben, had then devised a plan which called for me to move someplace warm and make just enough money to get by. The idea was to keep my earnings so low that the court could claim none of it, and convince my former partners to make a settlement offer. So far they hadn't made a move in that direction.

I started dating Beth Ann a few months after arriving in the Panhandle, and for a time she had found my novel lifestyle exciting. She was interested in the fact-checking work I did, but as a successful businesswoman she eventually began to question Mark's strategy. She'd gone so far as to refuse to meet him when he'd visited during the summer, and I had only healed that rift by finding steady employment with Daley & Associates.

"Oh," she now murmured, in mock amazement. "You didn't say it was a *missing* will."

"I really shouldn't be telling you any of this," I said as I turned into her driveway. That was true, but I needed a sounding board in my new job and so I sometimes shared things with Beth Ann. Although I liked Walter and Jimmy, back in Exile I had friends I consulted from time to time about the fishier aspects of my work. I didn't have anybody like that up in the capital, and confiding in Beth Ann had done wonders for our relationship.

"Who am I going to spill this to? I've never even heard of these people, and from what you're told me about them, I'm probably better off that way. Do you really think someone took the dead man's will while he was being rushed to the hospital?"

"To quote Jimmy Hanigan, I hope so. 'Cause if it disappeared before then, we might be looking at something a whole lot worse." Beth Ann had met Jimmy shortly after I took the job as his assistant, and had warmed to him immediately. We sometimes went on dates with him and his latest girlfriend, Mandy.

"It does sound strange that the man died from what amounts to a poisoning, just after everyone mentioned in his will was at his house." Beth Ann could identify the key issue in just about any problem, which explains how she could run a camera store all day and then teach classes two nights a week. "You said it was a birthday party?"

"His last, unfortunately." We were greeted at the door by one of Beth Ann's cats, and she squatted down to rub its ears. I squeezed past her, briefly running my fingers through her dark hair before beginning to empty my pockets on the hall table.

"It wouldn't be too hard to slip a few pills to someone at a party." She wrapped her arms around my waist from behind, powerful muscles for such a slim girl, before she continued to think out loud. "Different people mixing the drinks, maybe. Or maybe the old man had a special diet, something nobody else would get served."

I heard the words in my ear, marveling at how much of my job was rubbing off on my girlfriend. I let my head sag backward against hers, the tension slowly leaving my neck.

"Birthday party…maybe a cake, and even a few moments when the lights were turned out," I murmured, enjoying the embrace.

"I didn't think of that!" she exclaimed, letting go of me so fast that I almost fell over. "What about pictures? You should ask if anyone was taking pictures."

"I'm not sure I'm following all of this," I stammered, reaching for her again only to see her walk into the living room.

"Cameras? Photos? Remember what I do for a living? You should find out if there were pictures taken that night, and get copies. Or maybe even the digital file—"

"Digital? Did you say 'digital'? Miss 'I Wouldn't Be Caught Dead Using One of Those Things'?"

"Stop being silly. I mean it. I've been dying to help you on one of your jobs, and here's a chance. If you get the photos—or files—I can take them to my lab and enhance them. You never know, one of them might contain a clue."

"A clue? To what? Right now it's just a missing will. And maybe there weren't any cameras there that night."

"Nowadays there's always a camera. Even if it's one of those ridiculous cell-phone jobs." She stopped, switching with ease back into her earlier mode from the hallway. She stepped closer, and I didn't waste any time wrapping my arms around her.

"Make sure you ask tomorrow, Frank. Promise." She took my earlobe between her front teeth and held it. "I want to help. I need to help."

As you can imagine, I earnestly meant to ask that question at some point the next day. The only tough part was deciding when and how. I was supposed to be meeting with Pratt's daughter, Kerry, in order to learn more about the beneficiaries of his charity, so asking about the birthday party was going to take a little work.

I called ahead, just to make sure Belinda was expecting me, and learned that Kerry Pratt-Graham wouldn't be there for another hour. I was already on the road, and decided that a little small talk with Belinda could also shed some light on her late husband's financial giving. After all, Kerry might have been managing those funds, but Belinda had been married to the guy signing the checks.

She was out on the porch, watering the hanging plants, when I pulled up. She was wearing a yellow dress that was light enough to justify a sweater, and a pair of gray plastic glasses. She was standing on a three-step folding stool when I came up the walk, and greeted me like an old friend.

"Good morning, Mr. Cole. Kerry will be here in a half hour or so. Can I get you anything to drink?"

"No, thank you, ma'am. I'm fine."

"Really? I just brewed a fresh pot of coffee."

"Well, in that case, I'd love a cup." She stuck a hand out toward me, and I helped her step down. There were a lot of plants out on that porch, and the plastic watering can she'd been using was obviously quite heavy. She set it down on the deck's well-traveled planks and led me inside.

"Would you think me evil if I said that it's nice to finally have a visitor who isn't a relative? Kerry's been just a dear, coming by every day, but after a while it made me feel guilty, taking up her time like that."

"I'm sure she doesn't mind." We entered the kitchen, which was painted a blinding white. The countertop was covered with the flotsam and jetsam of everyday living, from magazines to envelopes and what was no doubt Belinda's purse. The refrigerator, a large double-door job, was covered with magnets and notes, one of which was the shopping list for the week. "I'm assuming Mrs. Pratt-Graham's work lets her take this kind of time off."

"Oh, don't be fooled. You should talk to her or Neil— her husband—about how much time they have to spend with their clients. All it takes is one bad story about the stock market on the TV, and their phones start ringing."

"I didn't think of that. Holding the clients' hands must eat up a lot of hours. Do you think that cuts into the time she can give to the charity?" It wasn't the most elegant segue, but Belinda was clearly in a talkative mood and I didn't want to waste it. Maybe she saw me as a neutral listener, or maybe she had indeed been hoping for a guest who wasn't related to her.

"It used to, but things got easier once she and Neil put their businesses under one roof. Now, when the charity pulls her away, Neil can step in for her." She stopped, holding the coffee pot in midair, and smiled. "Honestly, I sometimes think that those two treat their clients like the children they never had. You know—if one parent gets tied up at work the other one picks up the kids."

"They have no children of their own? I didn't know that." I knew that the son, Thomas, had kids, but had found nothing online to suggest the Grahams did or did not. Depending on the age, children can carry cameras to birthday parties.

"No, and I'm not sure they mind. Kerry takes after her father that way. Business comes first." She held up a sugar cube in a pair of tongs, and I gave her the two-finger sign. She continued speaking while dropping the requested pair of cubes into my cup. "You know, I think that if Neil wasn't in the same line of work as Kerry, he'd come second, too."

I wanted to pursue that comment without directly asking what it meant, so I said the next best thing, "I know what you mean."

"Maybe I came into this family too late to understand, but I always worried about the amount of time Kerry had to spend on that charity. Even in retirement, Chet wanted to know everything that was happening.

He'd call her at all hours of the night. Kerry told me he'd always been like that, always digging down to the smallest detail." She smiled in remembrance, and then motioned for me to follow her back toward the porch. "But she was always able to handle him, always had the answers ready, never lost her cool. She's made a huge difference these past few days, I can tell you."

We went back out onto the porch, and I handed the watering can to her once she'd gone back up on the step stool. Settling back into one of the rattan chairs, I took a sip of the coffee and continued to listen.

"I hope you don't mind me going on like this, Mr. Cole."

"Not at all. It's actually a big part of my job. And please, call me Frank."

"Thank you, and of course you should call me Belinda." She set about watering three plants that hung in a cluster, and spoke without looking at me. "Frank, do you think it's possible that Chet destroyed his will?"

That caught me a little off guard, but as it was one of the firm's bigger questions I felt I should try to answer it. "Anything is possible. I didn't know him, so I really can't guess. The real question here is—do *you* think he did?"

I had to help her down just then, and she took her time repositioning the stool. I was standing by dutifully, waiting to hand the now-lightened watering can up to her, when she just plain gave up on the household chores. She looked as if she was about to cry again for just a moment, but then simply walked the two steps to another chair and sat down. I placed the can on the deck and retook my seat without a word, giving her a minute to compose herself.

"I'm sorry, I'm not asking the right question at all. Honestly I don't care about what happens with the will. What bothers me is how many people believe Chet took those pills deliberately."

"Has anyone come out and said that?" I knew the police suspected this, and had wondered if the topic had been broached directly with the widow.

"The kids, of course. Kerry seems to think it might have been a terrible accident, but I think Thomas doesn't believe that at all." She took a long breath and let it out slowly. "He probably thinks I gave his father the wrong pills."

"What would make him think that?" I asked this in almost a whisper.

"Because of his reaction at the time of the first… attack. Thomas worshiped his father, and he really didn't handle the situation well at all. He broke down and cried right there in the hospital, even after they'd told us Chet would be all right.

"I tried to console him, but he gave me a look that would have melted a glacier. That's when I realized he held me responsible for what happened. As if I somehow should have known something the whole pharmaceuticals business didn't know.

"I was always very careful with Chet's health, Mr. Cole! I practically died myself when they said his attack was caused by his medication. And I cleaned out that entire medicine cabinet while he was still in the hospital. I threw away every pill in the house, just to be sure, and refilled all the prescriptions except for the one that caused the trouble.

"Of course the doctors gave him a completely different medication for that, so I have no idea how those other pills got into Chet's desk."

This was incredibly delicate ground I was standing on, and I wasn't sure how Walter or Jimmy would want me to proceed. I wondered just what a police investigator would make of Belinda's wholesale destruction of the pills from the earlier episode, now that her husband was dead from what was possibly the same drug combination.

"Let's back up, then. How was your husband's mood in the weeks prior to the party?"

"That's just it. He was such a tower of strength. Nothing ever bothered Chet. He always said that was how he made it in the business world—he didn't dwell on things. Once he made a decision, that was it. Take this will, for example. He knew I didn't want his money, but he tried to fix things so I'd get it anyway.

"When I found out about the first will, I told him to make a new one. He tried to argue with me at first, but when he saw I wouldn't budge he gave in. Then he decided to leave Kerry most of the estate.

"That decision didn't please anybody except Chet. We went through a rough patch there, but I honestly thought things were settling down again. Chet was so happy at the party. I wish you could have seen him. Everybody was happy at the party."

She had to stop and blow her nose then, which gave me a chance to question something she'd just said. "Excuse me, Belinda, but did you say nobody was happy with the new will? Even Kerry?"

"I'm sorry, Mr. Cole, but I thought Walter would have told you all this. I really had no interest in Chet's money at all. I didn't want it, and I didn't feel it was my place to suggest who got it." She teared up, and I waited until she was ready to speak again. "I wanted to grow old with that man. That's what I wanted.

"But somehow I still got caught in the middle of this. I think Thomas and his wife felt I was telling Chet who should get what. Thomas had been trying to win Chet's approval for so long—his whole life they tell me—that the new will really hurt him. I think he believes I told Chet to leave the money to Kerry, but the opposite was true. I wanted Chet to split the money evenly between the two of them."

"He didn't listen to you."

"Not on that, he didn't. Don't repeat this, but he told me that Thomas was no businessman, and that leaving him a lot of money was the same as burning it. I also think Chet felt he could trust Kerry to help me if I needed it."

"I can understand how the son would be upset, but why would Kerry be unhappy? She'd been administering his charity all this time, and she's a financial advisor. What was bothering her?"

"Frank, please remember this was all going on long before I got here. Walter will tell you that Chet was a strict parent, and so was Caroline—Kerry and Thomas's mother. Chet and Caroline came from poor families, and they didn't want their kids growing up spoiled. So

Chet tried to teach both of the kids all about money, and business, from an early age.

"Kerry's told me that Chet was harder on Thomas than he was on her. But something strange happened there—the more critical Chet became, the more Thomas tried to please him. I think that's why Thomas had so much trouble with his first restaurants—he was more concerned with what Chet thought than what the customers thought.

"Kerry went the opposite direction while she was still a teenager. She picked an out-of-state college, and then worked in Chicago for several years. Chet opposed every bit of that, but in the end he decided she was just making a point about her independence. He even said she picked Neil for a husband because there was no chance he'd become another Thomas."

"Kerry's husband didn't get along with Mr. Pratt?"

"No. You see, Kerry had a way of handling her father that deflected his criticism, laughing it off or making fun of it. And I think Chet respected her for that. But Neil isn't cut from that kind of cloth. If he doesn't like you, he lets you know."

"So how does that lead to Kerry not wanting the money she was already managing?"

"Chet and I dated for a year before he proposed, so I saw him and Neil snarling at each other more than once. Chet never gave up trying to control Kerry, and one time Neil accused him of putting her in charge of the charity so he could give her orders. It was a very ugly evening."

"But everyone was getting along on the night of the party?"

"Yes. That's the strange part. It was as if things had finally calmed down, as if everyone had just decided to accept the will as final."

A car pulled into the driveway just then, the same blue BMW from the day before, and I could see Kerry Graham at the wheel. She raised a hand in a modest wave, and we both returned it.

Standing up, Belinda put a hand on my forearm before speaking. "Thanks for listening to me, Frank. I know I was rambling, but I just can't get it out of my head that for the first time since I married Chet…I felt like everything was going to be all right."

CANDOR SEEMED TO RUN in the family, even though Belinda and Kerry were not related by blood. No sooner had Kerry arrived than she launched into her own questions regarding her father's death. I quickly got the message that the missing will was not half as important to either of them as the circumstances surrounding Chester Pratt's demise.

"You should have seen us, Mr. Cole," Kerry continued talking as we moved from the porch to a quiet side room. It was a spacious affair, with wood paneling up to waist height and then filigreed maroon wallpaper above that. Expensive armchairs and side tables completed what was obviously meant to be a place of repose. "Everyone had a great time that night, my dad most of all.

"The whole family was there, Belinda of course, me

and my husband, my brother Thomas, his wife Lindsay, and their three kids. My dad really loved seeing his grandchildren."

I felt a psychic push from Beth Ann just then, and decided to go for broke. "Maybe I can still see it, or at least a part of it. Were people taking pictures?"

Kerry gave me a strange look at that moment, but Belinda didn't let me study it. "Oh, yes! There were so many flashes when I brought out the cake, I almost couldn't find the table."

"I'd like to have a look at those photos, if it's all right with you. Who was taking them?"

"I think it was Lindsay. She was near the end of the table facing Chet." The memory of the party seemed to cheer Belinda, and she smiled just a bit.

"What do you hope to see in the photos, Mr. Cole?" Kerry asked in a tone mixed with curiosity and skepticism.

"Oh, you never know. At the very least I'll probably see a bunch of smiling faces. It may help to establish that the family was getting along." I decided not to add that a picture showing a smiling Chester Pratt, hours before he was believed to have killed himself, might suggest he'd done no such thing.

Kerry now showed that she was a mind reader as well as a financial whiz. "My dad was in a great mood that evening, Mr. Cole, and I'd seen him several times a week in the past months. You don't need pictures to know there is no way my dad killed himself."

"So what do you think happened, then?" I sounded like a psychiatrist on that one.

She shook her head while biting her lower lip. "I don't know. I've thought this over a thousand times. Dad managed his own medications, so I suppose there was a chance he just made a mistake. But that doesn't explain the pills we found in his desk. He kept his medicine upstairs, and he certainly didn't keep it in a sandwich bag."

"You mean this wasn't a pharmacy-issue bag?" I'd been on pain killers once, just after ramming my car into a vehicle which had been tailing me, and my pills had come in a heavy plastic bag.

"No. All of Chet's pills were in bottles, with labels." Belinda answered that one. "And what we found in the desk was a sandwich bag...almost like something you'd see on TV about drugs sold on the street."

"That bothered me, too. My father was a meticulous man in every aspect of his life. Even if he took those pills intentionally, I can't see him putting them in a sandwich bag like some...junkie."

Kerry's face had clouded over, and she seemed downright angry that she couldn't figure out the facts before her. Either she'd taken some acting lessons, or she honestly didn't know what had happened that night.

Belinda looked just as frustrated, and I decided that my initial assessment of the two women had been correct. They might be the only ones who knew the combination to the safe, but I would have bet what little money I have that they didn't know what had happened here.

That is, if anything *had* happened. We still didn't have a toxicology report, so there was a chance that Chester Pratt had never ingested the suspect pills at all.

Even so, I felt that his widow and his daughter deserved some kind of answer.

"Listen. Walter asked me to focus on the loss of the will, but that investigation could possibly shed some light on how Mr. Pratt died. Kerry, I still have to interview you about the recipients of your father's charity. But I'd like you both to try to think of anyone else who might have been interested in seeing that will destroyed."

They both nodded at me with a dull kind of hope, their sincerity reinforcing my belief that they wanted someone to look into this.

"One more thing, and this could be quite painful."

They just stared at me, but I could tell they knew what was coming.

"If we start looking into how those pills got into Mr. Pratt's desk, you may not like the answers we find."

"It wasn't anyone in the family, Mr. Cole," Kerry stated as if it were an inescapable fact. "We argued over the will, but no one wanted my dad to die."

Somebody did, I thought, but simply nodded instead of speaking.

FOUR

"WELL DONE, FRANK." Walter said this when I finished describing Belinda and Kerry's suspicions regarding the death of Chester Pratt. He turned to Jimmy, who was standing by the office window looking out at the picnic area. "I told you they'd open up to him."

"They would have opened up to me, too," Hanigan replied, turning to give Walter an indecent smile.

"That's what I was afraid of."

"What are you two talking about?"

Jimmy gave my shoulder a small slap as he came around to join me in front of Walter's desk. "It's a compliment, Frank. You've got one of those personalities that disarms people. They feel safe telling you things they might not share with, oh, the family lawyer or his lead investigator."

"So telling me to meet with Kerry about her father's charity work was all just a smoke screen?" Regardless of their praise, I was starting to get a little annoyed.

"Not at all." Walter was speaking again. "What did you find out about the people Chester gave money to?"

"That it's a dead end. According to Kerry, her father donated to a wide variety of causes and institutions, but not in huge amounts." I flipped open my notebook. "In fact, he was limiting the distributions because he wanted to grow an endowment large enough to be split off from his estate, something that would go on after he died."

"He mention any of that to you, Walter?"

"Yes, he did, when we were drafting his first will. We discussed the creation of a trust which would eventually grow into that endowment, but he was afraid it might mess things up if he died suddenly.

"That's another reason he decided to leave the bulk of his estate to Kerry, once Belinda put her foot down. He wanted her to be able to apply the money as she saw fit, either to help out the family or build the endowment."

"Help out the family? How? Things like paying for his grandchildren's college?" I asked, already half guessing the answer.

"More like keeping his son's business afloat. Thomas doesn't have the money smarts that Kerry does, and a couple of his other restaurants failed even with his father's help. His latest one is doing well enough right now, but Chester was afraid that putting his money in a charity trust might tie Kerry's hands if Thomas needed some assistance."

"Belinda mentioned that he wasn't much of a businessman. She said it was a source of friction between Thomas and his father."

Walter leaned back in his chair at this moment, looking first at me and then at Jimmy. "I know you two are usually careful about the firm's business, but this is personal stuff and I don't want it to leave this room.

"Chet Pratt was a demanding father. And his first wife, Caroline, was even tougher. Somewhere along the way to their first million they got this weird, dynastic attitude about their children. I've seen it before in wealthy families, and it usually works itself out when the kids go their own way, but that didn't happen for Chet.

"Kerry rejected the whole thing when she was a teenager. She wasn't a troublemaker, but after a certain age she just wouldn't do anything they asked." He gave a small laugh. "It's really been strange, watching her take more and more of a role managing the family money after rejecting it for so long. But even as she took on that burden, it was always on her terms.

"Thomas is the exact opposite. He wanted to live up to his parents' expectations, but he just didn't have the horse sense. That became apparent while he was still in college, but Chet never gave up on the idea. Over time it became a real sore point between them, and Chet was afraid that Thomas would see the latest change in the will as kind of a punishment."

"According to Belinda, that was the initial reaction. And get this, Kerry and her husband weren't happy with the new will either."

"Yeah, I'd sure resent it if someone tried to give *me* forty million dollars," Jimmy scoffed.

"Don't laugh," Walter answered gently. "Kerry turned Chet down when he first tried to convince her to take over the charity. And her husband was even worse. He and Chet never got along."

"That's what Belinda said. She even went so far as to suggest that Kerry picked—" I flipped a page of my notes "——Neil Graham for a husband because he wouldn't bow down to her dad."

"I don't know if I'd go that far, but Neil made it very clear, early on, that he didn't want anything from Chet." Walter cleared his throat. "Chet was a good guy, and a good friend, but he could be manipulative, as well. He wasn't above tricking people if that's what it took to get them under his thumb.

"He offered to buy the Grahams a house down here as a wedding gift, but Neil was dead set against it. He and Kerry got married in Tallahassee, but they went back to Chicago right after that. They were up there for, I dunno, a few years, and did fairly well. Chet told me that Kerry had hit some kind of glass ceiling in the financial community up there, though, and that he finally convinced her to come back down here where he could pull some strings for her.

"I don't think Neil was too happy about that. His business up north was doing well, but he relocated anyway. Chet got Kerry on to a board or two, pushed some heavy hitters her way, and so her practice really took off. Chet believed Neil resented that, and that Kerry fought against the new will because of Neil."

"Let me get this straight." Jimmy sat up in his seat. "We've got a son who was unhappy because he was only getting a fraction of the money, a widow who didn't want any of it and a daughter who was getting the lion's share who didn't want it either."

"Remember that's what we *had*. But here's what happens if we don't find the will—the widow who didn't want the money gets half of it, the daughter who didn't want the money gets a quarter, and the son gets a quarter, too." Walter explained.

"So we actually have three interested parties who might be happier with the will missing." Hanigan summed things up.

"How do you get three?" I'd just spent the entire day with Belinda and Kerry, and neither one of them looked happy to me.

"Regardless of what she says about not wanting the money, Belinda now stands to become one rich lady. Thomas benefits because he gets more of the estate than he would have under the missing will. Kerry and her husband are better off because they didn't want the money in the first place. They're still getting quite a chunk of change, but not as much as the old man wanted to leave them."

The three of us let that sink in for a moment. Intentionally or not, Jimmy had brought up a wrinkle which we hadn't considered before then: getting rid of Chester Pratt's will could have been the ultimate act of rebellion from either his daughter or his son-in-law. Destroying his will would allow them to ignore his final wishes on the earth.

"If that's true, it leaves us with an entire family who might have wanted to make that document disappear." Walter summed up, as if the statement were physically painful.

"And they were all together just a few hours before the old man ingested the pills that killed him." I had to add that, but instantly regretted it.

"I'm not willing to look at this as a murder, Frank. At

worst, it's an opportunity theft. Chet died, whether by accident or his own hand, and someone took his will in the confusion that followed." Walter stated this with an edge to his voice. "And as far as Belinda Pratt is concerned, I sat through the entire prenuptial discussion with her and Chet. She didn't want his money. Period."

"We really can't rule her out, Walter." Jimmy kept his eyes on the carpet as he spoke. "She has the combination to the safe, and who knows what was going through her head? She could have tossed the will in a fit of grief, not greed."

Walter seemed to think about that for a moment. "Who had the combination again?"

"Belinda, Kerry and Pratt himself," I answered, having given this fact considerable thought during the day.

"You don't necessarily need the combination to get into one of those safes," Jimmy offered, looking at the floor again.

"What are you saying, that someone ran out and hired a safecracker when they heard Chet was in the hospital?"

"I'm saying it's not impossible to get into one of those. That's all."

"I've been thinking about that," I began slowly, and both men rewarded me with their attention. "Password security was a bit of an issue for my old software company up north. My people were always writing their passwords down in obvious places, no matter how much we told them not to. If you walked through the office and lifted up random keyboards, you were likely to find slips of paper with the passwords right there."

"What's your point?"

"Most people remembered the passwords they used every day, but it was the codes they didn't use a lot that they were likely to forget. Those were the ones they wrote down. From what we've learned, I bet Mr. Pratt was the only one of the three people who knew the combination who went into that safe with any regularity.

"I should have asked this when I was there earlier, but I wouldn't be surprised if both Kerry and Belinda have the combination written down somewhere. I bet Kerry's is in her purse, and Belinda's is probably somewhere in the house. If it's written down, anybody could read it."

"See? I told you he'd bloom if we gave him time." Jimmy smiled broadly while waving a hand in my direction, and Walter smiled, too.

"You did indeed. Okay, let's stop guessing here. Tomorrow I want you to run down exactly who knew the combination. Find out if Belinda or Kerry shared it with anybody—you know, if they told someone just in case. Ask them if they wrote it down anywhere, and if they say yes, find out where that was kept.

"Emil has already arranged for you to meet Thomas Pratt in the afternoon, so I'll have him get you another session with Kerry in the morning.

"I'll call Belinda myself. Now, you two scram."

I WAS BEGINNING to enjoy the hours we were working on the Pratt case, because so far both nights had been free. I called Beth Ann, who agreed to a double date with Jimmy and his girlfriend, Mandy. We'd done this a few times before, and it had worked out well. After a quick shower and shave at Jimmy's place, we were back on the road headed to a nice Tallahassee restaurant, one of many where Jimmy knew the maître d'.

"One thing bothers me more than anything else here. As I've said before, it's not what you see, but what you don't," Jimmy confessed as I drove. "It's been almost two weeks since Pratt died, there's been no movement toward probate, and yet no one's complaining. I can understand Belinda letting Walter take the lead, if only because she really hopes we'll find the will. But the others, especially Thomas, should have been squawking by now. Maybe even getting lawyers of their own.

"And yet there's been nothing. It's almost like they're all afraid to make noise."

"Maybe they are. Pratt died under suspicious circumstances, and demanding his money before the toxicology results come back could end up looking very suspicious." I turned into the large parking lot of Jackie's, a popular night spot we'd visited before. "And if one of them did take the will, then he or she knows it won't be found. They just have to wait."

"I'm so proud of you, Frank. You're starting to think like a criminal."

Jackie's was a two-story building, its white brick face alternating with rectangles of brown wood that reached down to the sidewalk beneath amber half-moon windows. The front door was red, and I usually had to take a moment, even at night, to adjust to the low lighting once I stepped inside.

The bar was off to the left of the main restaurant,

and Beth Ann was waiting there when we entered. She emerged from the bar dressed in a tight-fitting set of black pants and a loose-fitting white shirt, and gave me a kiss even though she usually kept the public displays to a minimum.

"Hi, Jim. Is Mandy joining us?"

His cell phone went off at just that moment, and he stepped away to answer it. My hand was still on Beth Ann's back, and she didn't seem to mind the open intimacy. Hanigan laughed into his phone and came back with a twinkle in his eye.

"Mandy's hung up at work. She says she can meet us later at the Beat if you like." The Beat was Jimmy's name for The Beaten Ground, a coffee shop over by Florida A&M which often featured poetry readings. It was one of his favorite hangouts. "And since three's a crowd, I'm going to let you two enjoy a nice dinner. I'll just have something at the bar…"

"You'll do no such thing." Beth Ann took his wrist just before sliding her other arm around my waist. "Mandy would kill me if I left you alone in there. You should see some of the ladies that dropped in a few minutes ago."

Jimmy made a playful half turn toward the bar. "Maybe I should."

Beth Ann maneuvered the three of us to the maître d's stand, and I recognized the man who approached us even though I couldn't remember his name.

"George. Nice to see you again." Hanigan disengaged himself from Beth Ann long enough to slip George a folded bill while shaking his hand. "How about letting us have the back booth, and a little privacy? If you have to use the other booth, try to give it to somebody hard of hearing."

"Absolutely, Mr. Hanigan!" George probably would have had the same reaction even if his palm hadn't been greased. Jimmy Hanigan was practically a walking party, and bouncers, bartenders and people in George's position sensed this. "Right this way."

"FRANK, I CAN'T BELIEVE you violated the firm's code of ethics by discussing a case with an outsider." Hanigan leaned back on his side of the table, shaking his head at me and Beth Ann.

"I'll bet. Now just why did you ask for the back booth and some hard-of-hearing neighbors? So we could talk about sports?" We all had a small laugh at that, largely because Hanigan never shied away from discussing our cases in front of both Beth Ann and Mandy.

"Just trying to give you two a little privacy. I renew my offer to head on over to the bar and see if those wild women are still there." He was letting the Southern accent loose now, but it wasn't working on Beth Ann, who kicked him gently under the table.

"I already told Frank I'd be happy to look at any pictures from that birthday party. And I'm pretty good at tightening up the images in those things."

Jimmy gave me a long, appraising look. A wry smile played across his features, and Beth Ann misunderstood it.

"Hey, it was just an offer. Maybe you already have someone who does that for you."

"That's not why he's smiling, sweetie." I hadn't looked away, and could tell that Hanigan knew it was time for the big discussion. "Jimmy's just as suspicious of how the old man died as I am. No matter how many times we say we're just trying to determine what happened to the will."

Hanigan leaned forward then, and motioned us both to do the same. We'd been keeping our voices low, and so far George hadn't put anyone in the only other back booth, but there were limits even to Jimmy Hanigan's indiscretion.

"Okay. Walter is still hoping this was just an opportunity theft, but we got some new information today that might suggest otherwise. I spoke with a cop buddy of mine while you were at the Pratt house. There are still no results from the toxicology test, but the police held back some other information. They didn't tell the members of the family yet, so you have *got* to keep this to yourselves.

"The baggy they found in Pratt's desk drawer, the one that held the prescription drugs that gave him his first heart attack, had something else in it, too. Sleeping pills."

I lowered my hands to the tablecloth, my mind moving over the new revelation. Beth Ann looked at me without saying a word, and Hanigan leaned back as if waiting for me to speak. I didn't make them wait long.

"I wondered why Pratt didn't call for help when he first started having trouble that night, even if he was trying to do himself in. I figured it must have been a doozey of a heart attack, one that carried him away instantly, for him to be found slumped in his chair like that. But it still sounded strange."

The waiter appeared with the salads, and we gave him plenty of time to leave before Jimmy resumed the discussion.

"Right now it's all a big guess, until we get the tox test back. Who knows? Maybe nothing from that baggy was in his system at all. But you're right. If he started feeling chest pains, why didn't he reach for the phone or call for his wife?

"The cops don't think it supports foul play, though. Some of them even think it shows that Pratt killed himself—that he didn't want to be awake when it happened.

"But I don't buy that. Not with this much money at stake, and the way the will was missing right after. This whole thing feels like somebody's big plan to get rid of both the old man and the new will at the same time.

"And yes, Beth Ann, we'd very much like your help with the pictures from the party." Hanigan reached for his fork and knife, and began cutting into his salad. He stopped a moment later, a grin playing across his face. "In fact, with the number of potential suspects in this one, we may have to ask you to go undercover for us."

This abrupt suggestion was typical of Hanigan's free-wheeling style, but it was also news to me. "I don't think that's a good idea."

"Why not? You and I are gonna have to interview every member of that family. That makes it hard for us to tail them. If one of them sees us hanging around, they're gonna call Walter and complain. But who could complain about someone as nice as Beth Ann hanging around, particularly when they've never met her?"

"She's already got a job. Two jobs."

Beth Ann elbowed me just then, and not lightly. "Hey, mind if I answer for myself? Jim, what do you mean by 'hanging around'?"

"Oh, we're not talking about anything long-term here. What I mean is, sometimes we need a fresh face to step into a bar or a hotel lobby to see who's talking to whom. You'd be perfect."

"She would not. She attracts too much attention." Another elbow. "Because of her looks, I mean."

"Well, think about it anyway. I can already see your cover story—Job seeker, just interviewed for a position in a nearby office. A gal like that would have a lot of questions about what it's like to work in the surrounding area. Perfect icebreaker."

"That's stupid." It really wasn't, but I didn't like the look that was creeping into Beth Ann's eyes.

"Single mom." Hanigan continued. "Absolutely *has* to land this job. Instant sympathy. Make sure you have a picture of at least one little kid on you, or the whole act is blown right there."

"You sound like you've done this before." Beth Ann rubbed my thigh under the table, as if saying she wasn't really considering Jimmy's crazy idea.

"Absolutely. And they bought it, too. Until they asked to see the pictures and I didn't have any." He shook his head, biting his lower lip. "It was a shame. I really had them going. And I looked *good* in that dress."

LATER, WE MET UP with Mandy at the Beat and stopped talking for a good long while. The Beaten Ground was a standard college hangout during the day, with plenty of small tables, sofas and reading chairs, but at night it became more of an all-ages club. Heavy rugs were tossed all over the floor of the reading area, the lights were dimmed, and most of the time there was some kind of entertainment.

Some evenings they went down the Beat Generation trail (advertised as "Off the Beaten Path" night on the chalkboard near the door) with poetry recitals or readings from Kerouac fans. Other nights there was live music, usually quiet guitar stuff that I found quite enjoyable.

That night a series of poets, young and old, took turns standing in front of an open mike to let us hear their latest. I'd never had much time for this kind of thing when I'd actually been in college, and had been downright shocked to learn that a guy like Hanigan was a devotee, but it really grew on me after a while.

Of course it didn't hurt that I was sprawled on a well-used couch with Beth Ann using me for a mattress. Jimmy and Mandy occupied the opposite half of the sofa, and a dozen or so other couples had found similar uses for the rugs on the floor.

Mandy was a tall, thin graduate student with amazingly dark hair halfway to her waist. She claimed ancestry from a variety of continents, but her look was so exotic that it all fit. She was a little too tight-lipped for me, but Beth Ann liked her and that was really all that mattered. She was seated on the floor in front of

Jimmy, who was rubbing her shoulders but giving most of his attention to the stage.

The latest poet, a balding man in his sixties whose remaining hair was tied in a ponytail, was just finishing his set. I wasn't as well-read as the rest of the audience, but even I could tell he had a good rhythm and that most of his lines made a world-weary kind of sense. He received polite applause when he moved off, and I looked over at Jimmy to see he was still absorbed. As if sensing my scrutiny, he turned and gave me a thoughtful look in the darkness.

"I should have been born thirty years ago," he said wistfully, his eyes half shut.

"You were."

"I meant thirty years earlier. You know what I meant."

I did the math in my head. "You'd've been ten when the Beats were getting famous."

He nuzzled Mandy's hair, shutting his eyes briefly before another poet took the stage. "I would have fit right in. I've always been fast for my age."

The new reader was probably a college student, a dewy-eyed blonde wearing a flannel shirt untucked over a set of faded jeans. Her hair flowed down her back and shoulders, and her voice was soft and musical. "This one's called, *Fall Out of Thy Song.* I hope you like it.

Countless tugs hold my feet to the floor,
While your notes above and around me soar.
I leap, I reach, and still I long,
For the maybe meaning of your song.

Is the sun any closer, way up there?
Or, like you, does it refuse to share?
Is it the distance that makes you so dear?
And is that the reason you don't come near?

Like the coolness brought by an unseen breeze,
The pollen dust on the ardent bees,
The rain that drops from the heavy clouds,
Come, fall out of thy song, for now."

Beth Ann shifted slightly just then, pulling on my arm. "Tighter, Frank. Tighter," she murmured, and I forgot all about Jimmy, the case and the maybe meaning of the words.

FIVE

EMIL LEFT US a message saying that Kerry Pratt-Graham would be at her husband's office the next morning, Wednesday, and that we could meet the two of them there. Knowing that the Grahams had merged their businesses, I'd found it unusual that Emil referred to the joint office as her husband's. However, when we got off the elevator outside their suite the next day I saw that Emil was right. The wall outside the frosted doors held only the name of Neil Graham, Financial Advisor.

Jimmy and I had donned the jacket-and-tie outfits again, but nothing as formal as our first day with the Pratts. I wore a light brown suit made of a summertime fabric that breathed well but always seemed to need pressing. Jimmy wore a gray jacket over a white shirt and blue trousers.

We passed through the double doors and immediately found ourselves in front of Graham's receptionist. The carpet was tan, the walls were beige, and track lighting illuminated the small anteroom. The receptionist was a platinum blonde, chubby but attractive, seated behind a semicircular counter bearing the Neil Graham trademark.

"May I help you?" she asked in a friendly voice,

the very image of the caring trustee of other people's money. Or the doorkeeper for that trustee, at any rate.

"Yes. I'm Jimmy Hanigan and this is my partner, Frank Cole. Mrs. Pratt-Graham is expecting us."

"Mr. Graham is, too." The voice that said this came from our right, and was definitely male. I turned to see a tall, slim man approaching from what looked like the main office area. He stuck his hand out, but with a face that could have been carved out of stone.

He had a full head of brown hair, which someone had recently styled, and was dressed to look like a guy who knew how to handle money. He wore a style of dress shirt that I'd never liked, the ones where the collar and cuffs don't match the rest of the shirt. In this instance, the shirt was sky-blue, the cuffs and collar were white, and his tie was maroon. A gold chain held the tie in place, and a pair of gold cuff links gleamed in the light. His navy blue trousers reached down to tasseled black loafers, and I found that his ensemble made me wonder what he was hiding.

"Jim Hanigan, in-house investigator for Daley & Associates. This is my assistant, Frank Cole." Graham's grip was firm when he shook my hand, and his dark brown eyes tried to size me up. I didn't let them; after all, anyone can play the stone-face game.

"My wife won't be here for a few minutes. She's tied up in traffic. Why don't you come back to my office?" Graham told the receptionist to hold his calls, and we followed him down a short hallway past a pair of small meeting rooms where he probably explained investment strategies to his clients. Two offices faced each other at the end of the hallway, their wood-and-glass doors wide open. Judging from the decorating job in the one we didn't enter, I'd say that was Mrs. Pratt-Graham's.

As for Graham's office, it was done in Financial Advisor. He obviously wanted the place to be warm, but not so interesting that it might distract the clients. As we walked in I tried to latch on to anything that held my attention for more than a few seconds, and failed miserably. It was a corner office, and the view would have been good if it weren't sliced into tiny rays of sunshine by vertical blinds. Three framed paintings hung on one wall, but they were generic waterfowl shots. The other wall was taken up with a large bookcase, but a quick look showed that they were all legal tomes or investment manuals.

As if to confirm that he was, in fact, all business, Graham got right to the point. "I know you're looking for my father-in-law's will, but I think you're wasting your time."

"How so?" Jimmy asked this from over by the duck pictures. I had obediently followed Graham to his desk and sat in one of the two curved-back chairs in front of it, but Jimmy had not. He seemed fascinated by the paintings, but I soon saw that he was playing around with Graham's comfort zone. Rejecting the seat in front of the position of power, he was now roaming the office as if he'd been told to wait there all by himself.

"It seems pretty clear to me that he got rid of the thing, if it ever existed at all. It would be just like him to do something like that, too. He treated his estate like some sort of prize. He was always threatening to cut people out of his will, which is one of the reasons why I never bothered caring about it. He made certain members of the family jump through a lot of hoops that way, but not me."

Graham's tone of voice was really starting to grate on me, and I kicked myself for having taken a seat. His whole demeanor suggested a bored detachment, a know-it-all's snootiness, which I doubted he used on his clients. Even so, he was watching Jimmy closely as he moved around near the bookshelves.

"You think the will didn't exist?" Hanigan barely looked over his shoulder for that one, while tipping a leather-backed book up on one end as if inspecting its binding.

"I doubt you'd be here if your firm hadn't drafted something for him. But I never saw it, and couldn't care less if it's never found."

Jimmy turned around and walked slowly toward the chairs. "Why's that?"

"I didn't get along with Kerry's father, or her mother for that matter, and I don't want any of their money. So whether or not he destroyed the latest version of his will really doesn't matter to me at all."

"I guess you're doing pretty well here, then." Jimmy raised a hand as if to indicate the room around us. "A man would have to be rolling in it to say no to that kind of money."

"Not necessarily. And no, I'm not rolling in it. We're doing just fine, and we don't need anyone's help. But you're misunderstanding me. Chester Pratt was a con-niving guy, and one quick way to come under his thumb was to show an interest in his millions. Just talk to Thomas for five minutes and you'll see what I mean."

"*Have* you spoken to Thomas yet?" A familiar voice came from the door behind us, and I turned to see Kerry Pratt-Graham entering the room. She wore a sky-blue belted dress, and her brown hair was up. There was no way of knowing how long she'd been there, but she gave no indication of displeasure at her husband's commentary. She crossed the room to give him a kiss, and I noted that he made no effort to rise from his seat.

"Not yet, ma'am. We'll be doing that shortly." Jimmy turned to me with a bland look on his face. "Frank and I reviewed our notes last night, and came up with a couple more questions we wanted to ask. Should we move to your office?"

"I'm fine right here." Kerry sat on the side of her husband's desk, and I thought I detected a slight smirk from the desk's owner. "What would you like to know?"

I had my notebook out and open by then. "The other day I wrote down that there were four people with keys to the house—you, Belinda, your father and Thomas."

"That's correct."

"And you, Belinda, and your father were the only ones who had the combination to the safe?"

"Right. Thomas didn't have the combination, if that's what you're asking." She nodded at me as if we hadn't been on a first name basis the previous afternoon. In fact, her entire manner was different from the last two times we had spoken. She wore a smile of such pleasantness that it almost made her look stupid, and I already knew she was far from that. I didn't have time to ponder this much, and hoped that Hanigan had noticed the change in her behavior.

"Did you write the combination down anywhere? Just in case?"

"Yes, I did. It's on a slip of paper in my purse, and also on the inside cover of my appointment book."

"Did you tell anyone else the combination? Or that it was written down in those places?"

Kerry cocked her head to one side, as if trying to remember, and then turned to her husband. "Did I ever tell you I'd written the combination down?"

Graham looked ready to laugh out loud. "I can't see why you would. I never went near any of your father's things."

Kerry looked back at me, the issue settled. "No, then."

I looked at Jimmy to indicate I was done, and he picked up with a new line of questioning. "Mrs. Pratt-Graham, had you seen the actual will?"

"Of course I had. Dad showed it to me right after signing it. I was unhappy that he'd changed it, but there was nothing I could do at that point."

"Did you just look at it, or did you read it?"

The smile stayed, but the voice took on an edge. "Mr. Hanigan, I managed my father's charities for years before that will came on the scene. I read every legal document that had anything to do with his finances. Yes, I read the will."

Hanigan didn't look at Graham, even though he'd just proved the will's existence. He deftly changed subjects, a technique interrogators use to put people off balance.

"You were both at the Pratt residence when the plastic bag was found in your father's desk?"

Kerry answered for both of them. "Yes. It wasn't long after we'd returned from the hospital. Thomas and Lindsay were there, as well."

"Who found the bag?"

I might have imagined it, but a tiny bit of detachment slipped off of Neil Graham's face just then.

"Belinda found it when she and I were going through my father's study. I was emptying the safe, and she was checking the desk. She saw the bag when she pulled the center drawer open. She let out a bit of a screech."

"Why do you think that was?"

"I didn't have to guess, she told us. The medication that had almost killed my father was a very small, orange pill, and she recognized it. She said, 'I thought I got rid of those,' and then told us what they were. There were a lot of them in that bag."

"Did she touch the bag? Pick it up and look at it?"

"No. I stopped her. She was reaching into the desk when I told her not to touch it."

Jimmy nodded, processing the new information. "May I ask why you told her not to touch the bag?"

"I don't believe my father killed himself. Not now, and not then. When Belinda told me why she'd screamed, I suspected the pills were connected with my dad's death. His will was missing, and now we'd found something suspicious in his desk. We left them where they were, and called the police."

Jimmy slowly turned his gaze back to her husband. "Anything you'd like to add to that, Mr. Graham?"

"No. As usual, my wife's powers of observation far exceed my own."

"Thanks very much for your time, then. We'll be in touch if we find out anything new."

"'MRS. GRAHAM, HAD YOU seen the actual will?'" I read from my notes once we were in the elevator. "How is it that you can sound so much like a lawyer when you want to?"

"I've taken lots of depositions, Frank, and sat in on lots more. It rubs off on you."

"My old college roommate's a lawyer up in Manhattan. You remind me of him sometimes."

"Really? Is he tall, good-looking and wise beyond his years?"

"He's tall and good-looking."

We left the elevator and moved across the building's busy lobby. Outside, I was donning my sunglasses when Jimmy asked in a nonchalant voice, "See anyone you recognize?"

One of the things I like most about Tallahassee is how green the place is. Even in the middle of a commercial area like that one, you can usually find an expanse of foliage. Graham's office building faced a tree-lined park, and I pretended to stretch my arms in front of me while scanning the people on the benches. It didn't take me long to see the face that had caught Jimmy's attention.

"Oh, yeah. I wonder what he's doing here."

"Only one way to find out." Jimmy went down the steps with a purpose, and marched straight across the street toward a middle-aged man in a light suit and a white brimmed hat. Bob Barstow, a north Florida P.I. who had stepped on my toes before, was seated on one of the park's benches and pretending to read the paper.

Jimmy didn't stop moving until he'd taken a seat next to the older P.I., and I propped a foot up on the bench as if getting ready to tie my shoe. If this bothered Barstow, it didn't show.

"Jimmy." He was friendly enough when he said that, but his next syllable came out with considerably less warmth. "Cole. What's shakin', guys?"

"Oh, that's right." Jimmy was looking across at the building we had just exited, and I believed he was trying to determine if Barstow could see Graham's office from where he was sitting. "You and Frank don't get along. What was it? He showed you up on a murder case that made big headlines?"

"He didn't show me up. Everything I reported was the truth."

"Sure. Frank caught the bad guys, when you'd been out trying to prove the victim had it coming. You got in Frank's way, too."

"He tell you he put a nail under my friend's tire?"

Jimmy raised his eyes to meet mine, a broad smile creeping across his face. "No, he didn't. Shame on you, Frank! Leaving a thing like that off your résumé."

"Listen, guys, I like shooting the breeze as much as anybody, but I'm working here. You want to talk, we can meet for lunch or something, but in the meantime would you mind buzzing off?"

"Working? I thought you were retired, from the

way you were sitting here, readin' the paper. Whatcha workin' on, Bobby?"

"You know I'm not gonna tell you."

"Why not? Frank and I are looking into a missing last will and testament, involves a guy named Graham who works in that office building—" Jimmy pointed with his head "—right over there. That's why we're here. How about you? Who are you here to see?"

"It's a big building. Why don't you go look at the directory?"

"That's okay." Jimmy stood up, giving Barstow a playful slap on the shoulder. "Just wanted to make sure we weren't working the same case."

We started down the sidewalk toward the car, but Hanigan stopped after a step or two and turned back to Barstow. "We *aren't* working the same case, are we?"

Barstow only gave him a smile, and we headed off down the street. I had to believe that we hadn't come across the other P.I. by chance, and said so. "So much for wondering when the other family members were going to hire their own help."

"Right. But which ones?"

WHEN JIMMY WALKED US away from Barstow, it was in the wrong direction for going back to the car. I didn't say anything at first, not wanting to blow the act if it was for Barstow's benefit, but once we'd turned the corner of yet another office building I had to ask.

"Where are we going, Jimmy?"

"You're going back to Daley & Associates to get your car. Then you're going out to Belinda Pratt's place and asking her to tell you everything she can about the morning she found her husband's body. We need to know exactly where he was, what he looked like and anything else you can discover about the scene. Then find out where the baggy with the drugs was located in the desk—I mean exactly where—and anything else you can think of."

"That's some pretty sensitive stuff, Jimmy. I've already come close to making her cry with the other things I was asking."

"You spent a lot of time with her yesterday without giving her a breakdown, and she actually opened up to you. I know she's already answered these questions for the police, but we need to hear the story ourselves. Don't worry about it, I'll call ahead and let her know you're on the way."

"And what are you gonna be doing?"

"Watching Barstow, of course. I'm sure he's working the same case we are, but who's paying? And who was he watching there? Kerry, her husband, or both of 'em?"

"That would be pretty hard to do. One man watching two people."

"Don't be fooled, Frank. Barstow's not much to look at, and he draws some dumb conclusions, but nobody's better at nuts-and-bolts P.I. work. He's like an iron man when it comes to surveillance. He always works alone, he catches a few winks here and there, and he never gives up. We've used him before, and his work's been good.

"But you are right, one man can't tail two people if

they split up. So when he picks one of the Grahams to follow we'll have one of the answers we want."

"And the other answer?"

"That one might take a while. We need to know who hired him."

"CHET WAS SITTING right here in his favorite reading chair." Belinda stood in front of the large wing-back in Chester Pratt's study. She was holding up quite well, considering what we were discussing. The chair was near one of the windows, and a large floor lamp stood next to it. "It wasn't that unusual for him to sleep there. He had trouble dropping off most nights, and he loved to read, so it wasn't unusual for him to nod off down here while I was upstairs.

"Most of the time he'd come up later, but not always, so I didn't think anything was wrong when I woke up and he hadn't come to bed." She looked like she was misting up at that point, so I decided to give her a break.

"What did he like to read?"

"Oh, everything. He was an accomplished man. Did you know he spoke three languages?" She shook her head back and forth once, as if just learning of her husband's linguistic gifts. "He really enjoyed business books, though. He loved reading about people like the Rockefellers and the Carnegies."

I was scribbling quickly in my notebook, and made a quick note that I had stumbled across proof of Chester Pratt's interest in dynasties. "Was that what he was reading that night?"

This was a roundabout way of learning if the book

had been dropped on the floor when she found him, but I was trying to be subtle. It was an important question, as I still wondered how someone having a heart attack, even self-inflicted, could just sit there as it happened. I suspected this was why the police had withheld the information about the sleeping pills in the baggy found in Pratt's desk.

"Oh, no, he was reading Kerry's book, the gift she'd given him for his birthday." She turned to the boxes in the center of the room, and quickly found a large hard-backed book that was obviously quite heavy. I took it from her and immediately saw that this was no ordinary edition. Its cover was aged leather, its pages were dressed in gold, and it contained some absolutely beautiful historical maps from all over the world.

"This is quite a gift. You say Kerry gave it to him?"

"Well, it was from Neil and Kerry, but Chester told me after the party that he doubted Neil had had anything to do with it. Kerry knew her father loved old maps, and she really hit the mark with this one. He couldn't wait to get in here and start going through it."

I hefted it in both hands, surprised that I was already growing fatigued from holding it. "This is awfully heavy. Wouldn't he have been better off reading it at the desk?"

"Oh, he wasn't comfortable holding any book in the air for long, no matter what size." Belinda pointed to a low table near the reading chair, and for the first time I noticed it had wheels. "He would roll that in front of him and read off of it."

"Was that still in front of him…the next morning?"

"No. He would push it off to the side when he decided to shut his eyes. That's how I know what he was looking at. Kerry's present was on the table."

No matter how composed Belinda Pratt might be, I was quite uncomfortable with this assignment. She'd choked up a couple of times describing how she'd found her husband, and what I was going to wade into next would not be any more pleasant.

"I'm sorry to ask, but can you tell me where the baggy was found in the desk?"

She took a deep breath at that one, but it didn't stop her. We both walked over to the large block of wood which had been Chester Pratt's work area.

"We wondered if Chet might have been looking at the will and left it out, so one of the first places we looked was the desk. We found the…the bag in the center drawer, way in the back."

I sat down and pulled the middle drawer open. It was shallow, and moved smoothly on metal runners. I moved it back and forth a couple of times.

"Was there a lot of stuff in the drawer?"

"Yes, there was. Chet had a lot of keepsakes and little gifts people had given him, expensive pens and things like that. The bag was at the back." She was staring at the empty surface of the desk as if it were some kind of poisonous snake.

"I'm only asking because this drawer moves pretty easily. Do you think it's possible the bag was in the front, and that it slipped to the back when the drawer was closed?"

"Maybe. I don't know." She'd reached her limit, and

I kicked myself for taking it this far. Who cared if the bag was in the front or rear of the drawer?

"I'm sorry, Belinda. I really shouldn't have been asking all these questions. I'm just trying to get the whole picture."

"Frank?" Her eyes glistened, and she wasn't looking at the desk anymore.

"Yes?"

"If you do get that whole picture you're talking about, you'll be sure to tell me, won't you?"

It WASN'T ALL that late when I got out of there, so I headed back to the office to continue my online search for information on the Pratt family. Having met most of them, I felt I was now in a good position to interpret the more detailed information I now sought. Things were quiet at Daley & Associates, and so Emil was able to find me an unused cubicle off to the side where I could trawl the web.

Chester Pratt was a self-made millionaire who'd gotten his start selling farm tractors. His tale wasn't hard to find because just about every business club in the Panhandle had touted him as the classic rags-to-riches success story (usually in conjunction with a generous donation). He'd moved up quickly in the agriculture business, eventually getting his own company and branching out into everything from irrigation equipment to fertilizer.

He'd sold the business twenty years earlier, though, and pushed most of the resulting capital into the stock market. He'd done extremely well, and near as I could tell the bulk of his fortune came from his post-retirement investments.

His first wife, Caroline, had died of lung cancer after being sick for many years. That was five years ago, so Chester had spent three years as a widower before re-marrying. There wasn't much information online about the first Mrs. Pratt, except a shining obituary which had described her as a pillar of the community.

Kerry proved much more interesting. She'd gradu-ated first in her high school class before leaving the area for roughly ten years. She'd earned her undergradu-ate and her MBA from Northwestern, and her résumé said she'd worked in Chicago almost every one of those summers. Belinda had said this was an indication of Kerry's push-pull relationship with her father. Had she gone so far afield, and stayed there even when school was out, to show her father how easily she could evade his demanding grasp?

She'd met Graham at business school, where they'd been classmates. I dug around in his background a bit, and soon decided that Belinda had been right to be-lieve Kerry had one overriding requirement in a hus-band. Graham was an individualist, and unlikely to bow down to her father.

Graham had been the leader in everything he'd ever tried. Captain of the high school football team, president of his fraternity, even the captain of what must have been merely a club-level rugby team at business school. I got much of that from the biography he'd posted on his company website, and in one picture a supremely confident Neil Graham smiled at me from the center of a mud-spattered group of rugby players.

Perhaps he hadn't shown quite the stuff he'd need to survive Chester Pratt's connivances, though, because Kerry had kept him up in Illinois for the first five years of their marriage. She'd found a mid-level job at an investment bank there in Chicago, and Graham had started his financial-planning business working out of a house they'd bought in the suburbs.

They came to Tallahassee after that, and I checked the dates to make sure that Caroline Pratt had not yet become sick when her daughter came home. I wondered what had prompted this migration until I saw the high-paying gig Kerry had landed upon her return. She had jumped up several notches in the investment world, taking a position as a senior vice president with a well-known brokerage outfit. A little more digging showed that Walter had been right to suspect nepotism in that job hunt: Chester Pratt had sat on the company's board.

She'd risen quickly after that, and appeared all over the financial news in the years that followed. She was clearly some kind of whiz at finance, and seemed to have outdistanced her husband in their field.

What I was reading began to mesh with Kerry's odd behavior in her husband's presence that morning. Speaking to me at the Pratt house, she'd come across as a frank, intelligent woman deeply concerned about her father's demise. Sitting on her husband's desk, she'd appeared to be practically a cipher, almost playing with my questions until Hanigan had gotten a small rise out of her.

This fit the picture which Belinda had suggested, of a woman striking a difficult balance between two driven men. With Graham she seemed to play at subservience, even leaving his name on the office door when she was far more well-known in the financial community. I had no way of knowing how she'd behaved around her father, but she'd certainly used him when it was time to move up in the business world.

"I guess the domineering old man had his uses after all," I murmured to myself while reading off the screen. "You got your household together up in Chicago, trained Team Captain Neil the way you wanted him, and then decided to head home so dad could kill the fatted calf for you."

My cell phone rang, and I had to stop searching the internet for the day. Hanigan had found something, and wanted me to meet him at a local bar near Graham's office, a place called Clark's.

CLARK'S WAS AN upscale hangout, one of those bar-restaurants where white-collar workers go for a snort before heading home or deciding to stay for dinner. It was only two blocks from Graham's office building, and a steady stream of people in business attire came and went while I sat outside.

I'd called Jimmy once I was close, and been told to find a spot where I could see the front door. I'd tried a couple of different spaces in an open parking lot across the street until I found one that let me observe the comings and goings at Clark's. I shut off the engine after opening the windows wide to let in the early-evening breeze.

Jimmy hustled up shortly after that, and hurriedly indicated that I was to push over. He climbed in quickly, and fixed his gaze on the front door.

"Okay, Graham's inside but I think he's getting ready to leave. He came here with his receptionist—you know, the blonde—and two other gals who sounded like they work in the same building."

"Sounded? Sounded? You didn't go in there, did you?"

"I wouldn't learn very much waiting outside, would I?"

"But he might have recognized you!"

Jimmy's eyes slid around to give me a doubtful look, and he shook his head. "Not a chance. Nobody sees old Jimmy H when he doesn't want them to. I came in through the back door. Place is pretty dark, lots of booths where you can sit and watch, even a few little corners.

"Anyway, they're all up at the bar with their backs to the room. Graham's been looking at his watch, nursing one drink, while the girls have been puttin' 'em away at a steady clip. I figure he's got someplace to be, and should be leaving sometime soon." He fished his keys out of his pocket and handed them over. "My car's a couple blocks down from their office. I'm gonna tail Graham, see where he's going that's so important. When he's gone, I want you to go in there."

"What?"

"His receptionist isn't going to remember you, Frank. And you're not going to approach them anyway. Just find a spot nearby, and try to pick up on the chatter. They're a nice, loud group of girls, and I bet they'll start talking about Mr. Graham as soon as he's gone."

I wasn't ready for this. Jimmy was crazy to have gone in there while Graham was at the bar, and I was sure his Gal Friday would recognize me the instant I came through the front door. Unlike Jimmy, I had no idea of how to get in the back way.

"What do I do if I get spotted?"

"What every good P.I. does. You walk out. Not fast, not slow, and if someone thinks they know you, tell them they're mistaken. Wait, here he is. Get out."

I was standing by the car a moment later, watching Neil Graham as he walked up the sidewalk toward his building. He didn't seem in a rush, so Jimmy didn't start the engine right away.

"Jimmy, why are you tailing Graham at all? What happened to Barstow?"

"He didn't follow Kerry when she left the building a couple hours ago, so now we know he's tailing Graham."

I looked about me quickly. "Is he around here?"

"Doubtful. He packed up and left about an hour ago." He gave me a smile. "Hey, even the iron man has to eat. I'm guessing he's got Graham's routine down, and that he doesn't expect him to go anywhere special. But we'll see."

He drove off in my car just then, leaving me staring at the suddenly ominous front door of a local restaurant.

IF IT SOUNDS WRONG to you that Jimmy Hanigan decided to go inside Clark's, and then instructed me to do the same, you're not alone. Perhaps he was right in believing we wouldn't be recognized, and even if he was wrong there were plenty of excuses we could produce. We could say we'd been in the area all day and decided to wet our whistles. We'd heard Clark's was a nice place and wanted to check it out. We were lost and looking for directions.

Professional embarrassment wasn't the issue; the main risk here involved the cooperative attitudes of the Pratt and Graham families. We currently had access to everyone who would directly benefit from the loss of Chester Pratt's will, and all of those people had been at his birthday party the night he died. So far they were all willing to talk, even if they were just trying to avoid suspicion. Getting caught tailing them could have big ramifications as far as access was concerned.

In the meantime, it was just plain stupid. Jimmy had jokingly mentioned using Beth Ann for such an assignment the night before, but this is a genuinely good technique. Many P.I. firms maintain a stable of operatives, on salary or not, who can help out when the primary investigator is already a known face.

Unfortunately, "Jimmy H" hadn't thought of that. He had plenty of contacts who would surrender their cars to him on very short notice (myself among them, apparently) but when it came to inserting an eavesdropper into a place like Clark's his only option was to send me or go himself.

I began rehearsing my lines even as I crossed the

street. The sun was still high in the sky, and it seemed to redden the brick-front that made up the lower half of Clark's exterior wall. Bullet-shaped windows of murky brown glass rested on top of the redness, and I hoped it was just as hard to see out of them as in.

I could tell background noise was going to be a problem as soon as I came through the door. This was clearly a drinker's bar at that time of night, and the din wrapped itself around me. A coatroom was off to my left, and an unmanned greeter's lectern stood to my right. I put my eyes on the floor, and walked through the place looking like a guy who was trying not to be seen.

Hanigan was right about the booths that stretched out of eyesight, but the close ones were all full by then. I saw an archway farther back, which led to the dining area, but a waiter stationed there would probably ask me if I wanted a table if I chose to stand near him. I had to find another vantage point.

Just then a large man in a suit, his collar open and his tie askew, bumped into me as he passed. He had that determined air of someone who knows where the bathroom is, and so I followed him around the corner of the bar to another archway, which led to the privies.

This spot allowed me to look through a set of wooden rails atop a dividing wall, and I soon spotted the group in question. The platinum blonde receptionist from Graham's office was on a stool with her back to me, laughing at something another woman was saying. I quickly determined that the two women on either side of her were the friends Hanigan had mentioned, and that all three of them were becoming tipsy. Every seat at the bar was taken, but a nearby booth opened up right near them and I decided to go for it.

I still wouldn't have been able to hear their conversation, but I figured I could at least find out if they were regulars. A casual complaint to my server about the noisy trio might elicit advice about getting used to them because they were there every night. I was considering that ploy when a young couple raced past me on either side and stole my booth when I was no more than three feet from it.

I was also just a few feet from the people I was supposed to be watching, and now I had nowhere to go. I've been told that P.I.s tailing someone in a car have to be prepared to pull over and park at a moment's notice, but I hadn't expected to be put in a similar situation inside a bar.

I froze there for an instant, thunderstruck that my plan had so quickly gone awry. Panic swept through me when I saw I was standing right next to the people I was supposed to be watching.

There were no seats at the bar, and no open booths in front of me. I would have had to turn completely around to go looking for another, and would probably get spotted by Graham's receptionist in the process. I briefly considered reclaiming my vantage point near the restrooms before making a much better decision, one that mirrored the standard answer in a car surveillance when there is no place to park.

"Oh, to heck with this." I muttered as I got moving again, straight out the door and into the sunlight.

I HAD TO WALK AROUND Graham's building three times before finding Hanigan's car. Each time I went a block farther out, so the crimson flush I'd worn upon emerging from Clark's had plenty of time to dissipate.

I moved the car back to the same spot across from the restaurant where I had parked earlier. The platinum blonde and her cohorts hadn't looked ready to leave the place anytime soon, and finally one of my hunches turned out to be right. I got to sit there for another hour before they came out the door. The sun was setting by then, and they seemed to have mellowed somewhat since I last saw them. They headed back toward Graham's building, and I decided I could make a fair amount of money taxiing people back and forth between the two establishments. After all, I now knew the area.

Jimmy had wanted me to collect some scuttlebutt from the women, and so I decided to make one last effort. Clark's was still busy when I went in this time, but much of the crowd had shifted to the dining room and so I sat at the bar in what had been the receptionist's seat.

"What'll I get you?" asked one of two male bartenders. This one was a tall, beefy guy with a fringe of brown hair around his ears. He wore a short-sleeved maroon shirt with the word 'Clark's' embroidered on his chest in yellow, and I pegged him as one of those alcohol purveyors who knows a lot about his patrons.

"Dewar's. Neat." This is not my usual drink, but it's on the expensive side and I wanted an excuse to tip heavily with some of Daley & Associates' money. Things were slowing down at the bar, so I took my time getting my wallet out when he came back.

"I was in here just a little earlier, when the place was packed."

"I know. I saw you."

My face grew hot again. I'd been spotted by a guy serving drinks to a crowd two-deep at his bar, and I hadn't been in there even ten minutes. It rattled me, but I plowed on.

"There was a blonde lady here with a couple of gal pals. They come here often?" I tried to distract him by dropping a ten on the bar. "Keep the change."

He gave me a slight smirk at that, and I was sure he'd made me as a cop or P.I. Actually, I couldn't have been more wrong. He snagged the sawbuck and flashed a sympathetic smile. "They're in here most nights, a little after five. Next time just walk up and introduce yourself. Don't freeze up like you did. She's single, and she's looking. It'll be fine."

I didn't even touch the drink. When you've embarrassed yourself that badly, it's time to call it a day. Before you make it worse.

WE MET THOMAS PRATT at his restaurant late the next morning. He seemed genuinely affected by the loss of his father, and I didn't think it was an act.

I'd pulled some reviews of his restaurant, and most of them had described the place as sophisticated. Perhaps that had been a reference to the clientele or the cuisine, because the furnishing was all aged-wood-and-stucco. The floor was some kind of dark wood, and pillars separated the dining area into quiet booths further obscured by potted plants. It reminded me of Jackie's, except that Thomas had named it Lindsay's Place after his wife.

We got there just before lunch, but Lindsay's Place was only open for dinner and so the restaurant was just waking up. Thomas had been expecting us, and was standing outside smoking a cigarette when we pulled in. It was hot by then, and I was happy to be ushered into the shadowy interior.

Thomas Pratt stood a couple inches under six feet, but he probably didn't weigh a hundred forty pounds. His black hair was thinning slightly, and he was wearing two pieces of a gray three-piece suit when we met him. His shirt was white and recently dry-cleaned, and the watch on his wrist looked expensive.

"It feels like this is never going to end, you know?" he observed once we were seated in a booth with a window. A set of flimsy shutters had been pulled back to let in the light, and Thomas absently began straightening up some paperwork that had been spread across the white tablecloth. I had plenty of time to identify the papers as the restaurant accounts, and even when he'd gotten them together he didn't take them off the table.

"I'm sure this is a very tough time for you and your family, Mr. Pratt." Jimmy had shifted back into empathy mode. "We're only trying to determine what happened to your father's will, and recover it if possible."

"That's what Kerry told me. Gosh, I hope you can resolve this. I've got my hands full here at work, my second kid just started school, and with Pop's suddenly going like that..." He shook his head and then simply stopped, as if a spot on the tablecloth had caught his attention.

"I understand. We'll try to make this as quick as possible."

That seemed to wake him up, as he almost jumped in his seat. "Oh, no, that's not what I meant. I really want you to get to the bottom of this, so whatever I can do, or however long it takes, let's go ahead and do it."

"All right." Jimmy glanced at me, but I already had the notebook out. "We've spoken to your sister and your stepmother, of course, so some of this is just to confirm what we've already learned. I understand you don't know the combination to the safe where the will was kept."

"That's right. I really have no need. Kerry worked closely with Pop, but I don't think I've ever seen the inside of that thing."

"All right. We're trying to establish the events when your father went to the hospital." I had to hand it to Jimmy. He was discussing the sudden death of the man's father, and yet he'd chosen words that made it sound like a trip to the emergency room that had turned out to be nothing. "Mrs. Pratt called your sister, who went to the house and then to the hospital with her. They called you from there?"

"That's right. I'd just come back from dropping the kids off at school when the phone rang. Unfortunately, Pop was already gone by then, but Lindsay and I wanted to get down there anyway. We called Lindsay's mother, and she took Tommy, my youngest. We went to the hospital from there."

"Where do you keep your key to your father's house?"

"With all the others." He reached into his pocket and came up with a well-stocked key ring, which he laid on the table. "That's it there."

"Can you recall anyone asking you about your key, or about the combination to the safe?"

"No." He shook his head. "Not even members of the family. It just wouldn't have come up."

"Mr. Pratt, I understand this is a touchy subject, but how did you feel about the will?"

"Well, I was hurt at first. Very hurt. But Pop took me aside and explained that he had told Kerry to set up some kind of an endowment after he was gone, and that he wanted to make sure she had the funds to do that.

"And then I spoke with Kerry, and she promised me that I'd have help with the kids' college money if I needed it. That was pretty much my only concern."

"Pretty much?"

"Well, of course it bothered me that Pop gave almost all of it to Kerry. I know that he didn't have much faith in me as a businessman." He brightened just a little. "But look around you. We've been operating for over a year now, and we're still in the black. That's a big milestone for a restaurant, a year.

"And Pop lived to see that. I can't tell you how proud I was, the night we celebrated the end of our first year, with a big dinner right here. That was a good night." He dropped back into another chasm as a second thought came close on the heels of the first. "The birthday was another good night. We all had fun, and everybody was getting along for once. I gotta tell you, the next morning was a real punch in the stomach."

"I can imagine." Jimmy's words were barely audible. "We were hoping to see some of the photos from the birthday party. I understand your wife took some."

"No, no, Lindsay hates cameras. You're thinking about my oldest, Margie. She's got one of those digital jobbers, takes pictures like a pro. You'd like to see them?"

"If it wouldn't be too much trouble."

"Sure. I'll call my wife and ask her to download them from Margie's camera. If you've got an email address, we can send them right to you."

"Actually, could we get the whole camera?" I tried not to blurt that out, but I knew Beth Ann wouldn't want to start with files that had been downloaded and then passed through email systems. Both men looked at me strangely, so I tried to explain myself without admitting we planned to enhance the pictures. "It's better if we start with the original file, that's all."

"Okay." Thomas Pratt accepted that the way he'd accepted everything else we said, and took a cell phone from his belt. He started telling his wife that we'd be by to collect the camera, but it sounded like he'd called home at a bad time. "—because they want to look at the pictures from the party…heck, I don't know…"

He took the phone down from his ear and cupped it to his chest with a besieged look on his face. "Would you guys mind giving me a minute here?"

We slid out of the booth and walked over to the vacant headwaiter station near the door. Jimmy motioned me to keep silent until one of the staff had finished setting a nearby table, and then he leaned in close.

"That was a good catch, Frank, asking for the whole camera. But we have to be careful here. I think Pratt's still in shock from the loss of his father, so he's not picking up on why we're interested in the pictures. Right now, his wife is probably asking why we want to see them."

I glanced back toward the booth, and saw Pratt speaking and nodding with the same look of dejected resignation that he'd shown through most of our discussion. He finally ended the call, but instead of signaling us to come back he simply put the phone on the tablecloth and stared at it for a long while.

"Mr. Pratt?" Jimmy could have been imitating a nurse at an old folks' home, gently waking a guest. Thomas Pratt looked up without any trace of surprise, though, and I decided that he'd been kicked so many times in the previous weeks that nothing was making any sense to him anymore.

"I'm sorry, I just…seem to get lost in thought these days." It was more of a statement than an apology. "Can you come back in an hour or so? The house is a mess and Lindsay said she'd drop the camera here."

WE GOT SANDWICHES for lunch and ate them on a park bench far away from prying ears. The previous day's events had moved pretty quickly, and this was the first chance we'd had to catch up. I had a few questions of my own, but as usual I let Jimmy take the lead.

"Let's recap a little here. You notice anything weird

about the way Kerry was acting in her husband's office yesterday?" he asked, reaching for his soda.

"Yes, I did. It was like she was a completely different person. I think it was because her husband was there."

"Yeah. That's what I thought. I only got to speak to her the day we went over to Pratt's place, but you spent more time with her. What was she like then?"

"She was pretty outspoken about what happened to her father, insisting there was no way he could have killed himself. But in Graham's office she acted like we were wasting our time. What do you make of that?"

"It struck me as very odd, the way they played off of each other. Did you see how she sat down on Graham's desk like it was the hood of his car? Captain of the football team and the head cheerleader." He looked over at a distant game of Frisbee for a moment. "What was it Belinda told you about Kerry and her dad? That she knew how to handle him, deflected what he said?"

"Yeah. She also said Pratt believed Kerry picked Graham for her husband because he didn't get along with him."

"Right." He turned that over in his head. "But how's this for an explanation—what if what we saw yesterday was just their professional dynamic? Maybe they batted the questions back and forth so that neither one would be surprised by what the other was saying. They might have learned to do that as a reaction to her father, but is it possible they do that for everybody?"

"I hadn't thought of that. And we were in their offices, too. In that setting, they're normally chatting up people who are looking for an investment counselor.

So the playful husband and wife act might have come from their surroundings."

We both found a reason to take large bites of our sandwiches then, and long drinks.

"Okay, let's set that aside for now. What did you make of Pratt Junior?"

"He reminded me of me, back when my business was unraveling. Poor guy doesn't know which end is up."

"That's what I saw. Think it's an act?"

"No."

"Me, neither. Walter said Thomas never really measured up to his dad's expectations, and I think his old man's passing hit him like a ton of bricks."

"So you think we can rule him out? He does have a key to the house."

"He does at that. And there was a break in time, between the phone call and his arrival at the hospital, when he could have gone there. Who knows? Maybe he was out of his head over the news, and did something foolish."

"He doesn't have the safe's combination."

"He *says* he doesn't. We already proved that Kerry wrote the combo down, so that's at least one way he could have gotten it." He began stuffing used napkins into the bag that had contained his lunch. I took this as a sign we were leaving, and began draining my soda. "But I think you're right. He was floored by the loss of his old man, and I think he doesn't give a hoot if he gets a dime of his money."

His cell phone rang just then, and he flipped it open. A brief discussion followed, and it was clear he was talking to Thomas Pratt. Jimmy's face clouded over as he ended the call, and he gave me a look of helpless good humor once he'd put the phone away.

"That was Thomas. Seems little Margie took the camera to school today. We won't be getting the photos from the party until tomorrow."

SIX

THIS IS A GOOD SPOT to comment on the impetuous side of Jimmy Hanigan's nature. He was a skilled investigator, and could follow an interview strategy like nobody's business, but there was another side to him that didn't follow plans well at all. This was a bonus when we were confronted by unexpected developments—like the jogger the other day—but it also had the potential of getting us in hot water. I'd seen him approach dangerous suspects before, seemingly on a whim, and had not yet grown comfortable with that part of his psyche.

I got to experience some more of that discomfort that very afternoon, when we sat outside the home of Thomas and Lindsay Pratt for an hour while waiting for the Pratt kids to come home from school.

"Walter is going to have our butts for this," I said for the umpteenth time while looking up and down the quiet residential avenue.

"Remember…no matter how much he bites off, it always grows back." Jimmy spoke in a soothing voice, his eyes fixed on the Pratt residence. For a struggling restaurateur, Thomas Pratt sure had a nice place. A lush green lawn rolled down to the sidewalk from a two-story yellow-colored house with a massive bay window and a two-car garage. The houses around it were equally nice, and we had watched Lindsay Pratt drive off in an expensive Saab just a few minutes earlier.

Jimmy was sure she was going to pick up the kids, and no amount of arguing was going to get that out of his mind. Pratt had told us that his middle child had just started school, but it was the oldest, Margie, who allegedly owned the camera. Distant memories of kindergarten told me that the two children would be on different schedules, and I was even hoping that Margie had some kind of after-school activity, which would save us from confronting her mother.

"You know she's gonna call her husband if we knock on that door. And that'll be the end of his cooperation, right there."

Jimmy gave a small laugh. "Yeah, but look at it this way, if that was an act back at the restaurant, his reaction to this could blow it sky-high."

The Saab came back down the street, and once again my prayers went unanswered. Blond-haired and pigtailed Margie Pratt sat proudly in the front seat next to her mom, and the younger Pratt, a brown-haired boy, bounced excitedly in the backseat.

We watched the garage door rise on command, and I was surprised when Jimmy let it roll down behind the car.

"Aren't we hoping to prove the kid didn't take the camera to school?"

"Not at all. We want to get hold of it as soon as possible, and catching Mrs. Pratt in a lie isn't gonna help us do that. We'll give them a few minutes to put the schoolbags down, break out the juice boxes, and then we'll knock."

"And say what?"

"That we were in the neighborhood and thought we'd drop by, to save Mrs. Pratt the trouble of remembering to give the camera to her husband tomorrow." The words flowed from his mouth, and sounded perfectly reasonable for almost a full second.

"You expect her to believe that?"

"No more than we believed the camera went to school today. You heard the start of Pratt's conversation with his wife. She was *not happy* to hear that he'd volunteered the camera. She came up with the excuse about the house being a mess, and then thought of a better one that would keep us from getting the thing until tomorrow.

"Unless I miss my guess, she reviewed every one of those pictures just after hanging up on her husband. She saved them to her computer, and then thought *real hard* about deleting most of them from the camera."

"So why are we here?"

"To get a good look at her face when she answers the door and finds out who's come calling." He smiled again. "And if she hasn't deleted the photos yet, you're gonna see one deeply conflicted woman standing in front of us."

He opened his door, and swung a booted foot onto the street. "Come on, Frank. This is the fun part of what we do."

That turned out to be a lie, because Lindsay Pratt was—predictably—unhappy to see us. Jimmy put on his best welcome-to-the-neighborhood face, and I tried to melt into the bricks of the Pratts' front stoop as the door opened.

"Hello, Mrs. Pratt. I'm Jimmy Hanigan from Daley & Associates, and this is my assistant, Frank Cole. I believe your husband called about us." He didn't give her a second to respond, his eyes wide and friendly as he studied her reaction. "We were in the area, and thought we'd drop by to see if your daughter had brought her camera home from school yet. We were hoping to save you the trouble of getting it to us."

Whatever reaction Hanigan had hoped to elicit, I'm quite sure he got more than he bargained for. Lindsay Pratt was probably thirty-five, and the stone face that had answered the door didn't get any friendlier. She was a slim, attractive woman with brown hair pulled up on the back of her head and dark eyes that narrowed considerably in the instant before she spoke.

"How did you get my address?" The words were loud, but she wasn't shouting. This was someone who was used to telling other people what to do. "My husband told you you'd get the camera *tomorrow*. Now what are you doing here, interrupting my afternoon?"

"I'm very sorry if we've disturbed you, Mrs. Pratt, but we only wanted to save you the trouble of getting the camera to us." Jimmy could have had a very successful career as a door-to-door salesman. "Has your daughter come home yet?"

Her eyes opened wide, and this time I did expect her to start shouting. She knew darn well we'd been waiting, and now she was confronted with a question she didn't know how to answer. I had no idea why she'd wanted to delay handing over the photos, but it was going to look awfully suspicious if she refused to give us the camera.

"My daughter's schedule is none of your business, Mr. Flanagan."

"Hanigan."

"As if it makes a difference. You wait right here, the both of you. I'm calling my husband."

The door fairly slammed in our faces, and Jimmy flashed me a mischievous grin. I simply stood there in mortified embarrassment, and waited for what I knew was going to be a veritable hurricane of abuse.

True to her word, Lindsay Pratt had her husband on the phone when she returned. She was holding a large cordless device to her ear, and lightning seemed to be going into the receiver.

"They're right here, right on the doorstep! Now you make them go away! Right now!" And yes, now she was shouting. She stuck the phone out to Jimmy in one sharp, accusatorial movement, and he took it without hesitation. He showed even less reluctance when he turned and handed it to me.

"Speak to Mr. Pratt, Frank," he ordered curtly, and I took the phone from his hand for reasons that I cannot name, even to this day. Jimmy turned back to Mrs. Pratt without another word, and I stood there looking at the device like it was a live grenade.

"Hello? Hello?" I heard Pratt's voice, and brought the receiver up to my ear while Jimmy resumed his offensive.

"I really am sorry that we've upset you, Mrs. Pratt, but we honestly only meant to help out—"

"Stop saying that. Do I look like I need help?" Lindsay had recovered her bearing, and now launched into a low-voiced assault on Hanigan's politeness, intelligence, and even his family background.

"Hello? Is anyone there?"

"Hello, Mr. Pratt, this is—" *I can't believe I'm saying this* "—Frank Cole. I'm so sorry for the misunderstanding, but we were in the area and thought we were saving everybody a chore by deciding to drop by. Please accept my apologies."

Pratt sounded more flabbergasted than angry. "Mr. Cole, I really don't know what's going on here. This isn't what we discussed at all. I told you to come by the restaurant tomorrow, and that I'd have the camera for you then. And how *did* you get my address?"

Finally, a question I could answer. "It was in the file at the firm, sir. Again, we only wanted to help out here—" That phrase didn't go down any better with Mr. Pratt than it had with Mrs. Pratt.

"Help? Help? Do you hear my wife? Because *I* can hear her." A voice came over the receiver just then, and I had an image of someone at the restaurant approaching the owner with a question. We were, after all, coming up on the dinner hour. Pratt spoke to the new voice in a mumble, and I stuck a finger in my ear to blot out Jimmy's attempts at mollifying Mrs. Pratt.

"Listen, Mr. Cole. I don't have time for this. Please put my wife back on." I didn't think things could possibly get worse, but they just had. At least Thomas Pratt was being civil, but now I had to hand the phone back to his wife. Given the choice, I would have preferred to stick my hand in the tiger cage at the zoo.

Jimmy was losing ground fast, though, and so I screwed up what little courage I had left and passed the phone over his shoulder toward Mrs. Pratt. "Mrs. Pratt, your husband wants to talk to you."

She turned those dark eyes on me, and raised her eyebrows in mute outrage. Without a single word, she snatched the phone from my hand, took a step back into the house, and slammed the door again. Jimmy twisted his torso to put his back to the door's peephole, and then brought a finger up to his lips. Turning back to face the door, he clasped his hands together and assumed the expression of an undertaker listening to his favorite hymn.

The door didn't open again for a good five minutes, but we didn't move. It was still hot outside, and I felt a trickle of perspiration snaking its way down my spine just as I detected the sounds of someone approaching from inside.

Lindsay Pratt opened the door and stuffed a small, silver box into Hanigan's waiting hands. He didn't move, however, and neither did she. A moment or two passed, and then he spoke.

"Thank you very much, Mrs. Pratt."

"You two get off my property right now. And if you ever come back, I'm calling the police."

I felt a good breeze when she slammed the door for the last time.

WE GOT BACK TO Daley & Associates shortly after five, but as usual the place was still busy. There was almost always one team or other working on a big case, and in the months I'd been with them I'd never seen the building empty.

Jimmy stopped and quizzed one of the receptionists about something that I couldn't make out, and then joined me in the hallway leading back toward Walter's office.

"It's like I figured. Thomas ratted us out to Belinda, and she called Walter to say she didn't appreciate our little escapade." I was about to contest his choice of the word 'our' when he put me safely on the sidelines. "Take the camera to Conference Room B and download it onto the big screen there. Have a good look at every picture, and write up a list of what's going on in each of them. We want to be able to tell Beth Ann which ones to enhance and which ones to ignore."

"You're going to see Walter?"

"Hey, dropping in on Mrs. Pratt was my idea, not yours. It was a good decision, and it got us the camera, but like everything in the world, it has a price." He smiled like a kid who was used to being hauled into the principal's office. "Don't worry about it. This is the job. We step on some toes from time to time, and Walter will understand once I tell him she was holding out on us."

He started off down the hall when I thought of a question. "Hey. What am I looking for?"

"Somebody dropping pills in the old man's drink. What else?"

ALTHOUGH I FIGURED he was kidding about that, I was still eager to look at the photos anyway. Two of the firm's younger lawyers were just finishing up their take-out dinners in Conference Room B when I walked in, but they vacated the place when I told them I had to use the projector. My technical background came in handy at this point, and in no time I had a large photo of the extended Pratt family up on the wall.

This was a classic posed shot for the family album, and everyone except the photographer was in it. Pratt himself had been a bald man with glasses, and he had not been looking well in that particular shot. He and Belinda were seated in the center of a small gold couch, with both of Thomas Pratt's male children. The youngest, a blond-haired boy who looked to be about four, was sitting on Belinda's lap while the other one, the boy I'd seen in the backseat of Lindsay's car, sat next to his grandfather. Neil and Kerry Graham stood behind the couch with Thomas and Lindsay Pratt, so presumably the picture had been taken by the eight-year-old Margie Pratt.

That seemed to be proven by the next shot, because the young girl from Lindsay Pratt's front seat had joined the grandparents on the couch and Lindsay Pratt was no longer in evidence. Thomas Pratt looked a little lost, standing there by himself, but everyone was smiling and it appeared they were having a good time.

This was followed by several pre-dinner scenes, shots of the women getting things together in the kitchen and the men talking in the living room. I was a little surprised to see Neil Graham engaged in what looked like friendly conversation with his domineering father-in-law, but then remembered the oft-repeated opinion that everyone had been getting along that night.

The magnified pictures showed a lot of detail, and I had just begun to wonder how much work was left for Beth Ann when the party shifted to the dinner table. The Pratts had a dining room that I had not yet seen, and the lighting was not as good there as in the other rooms. A large chandelier threw strange light waves across those shots, and at first it was hard to determine where everyone had been seated. I'd been taking notes as directed, and now began to sketch out the rectangular table on a separate sheet of paper.

The table was long, and Chester Pratt was seated at the end farthest from his granddaughter the photographer. Belinda Pratt was nowhere to be seen, so I assumed she was at the end of the table facing her husband, probably getting elbowed by Margie as she worked the camera. Kerry Graham sat to her father's right, and Thomas sat to his left. Looking at a couple more shots told me that Neil Graham sat to his wife's right, and that the eldest Pratt son sat next to him.

An odd, snakelike image floated in the air on the right-hand side of one picture, and it took me a while before I recognized it as a spoon. A little closer scrutiny revealed a child's hand holding the utensil, and I was finally able to surmise that the youngest Pratt son, seated in a high chair, had been waving the thing in front of the camera. As if to help me, Margie changed her vantage point in the next shot, which showed Thomas, his wife, and then the spoon-wielding toddler on their side of the table.

The meal must have taken precedence then, because the picture-taking ceased until the moment when the cake was being brought out. The room was almost completely black with the lights turned off, and the candles on the birthday cake did more harm than good when it came to making out who was doing what. Chester Pratt's beaming face was illuminated quite clearly because the cake was placed right in front of him, and I recalled Belinda saying she had carried it to the table. In the next photo a still-seated Pratt was giving his wife a peck on the cheek, confirming she had been the cake-bearer.

It was hard not to smile at the scenes before me, even knowing the tragic events of that night and the following day. I was trying to make out who was standing near Pratt when the door to the conference room opened behind me. I expected it to be Jimmy, but was surprised to see the moon-faced Bernie Kaplan instead.

"I'm sorry, Bernie, but I'm using the room," I said, annoyed that there was no way to obscure the photo on the wall.

"That's okay. I just wanted to ask what you and good old Jimmy did to get Walter so worked up." Kaplan was wearing his usual smug look, and for an instant I wondered if he was just a scrunched-down version of Neil Graham.

"I doubt he's all worked up," I said, walking to the projector and switching it to a bulb-saving mode that blacked out the image. "Walter doesn't get excited about too many things."

Kaplan smiled at this. He appeared to be in the middle of something, as his shirtsleeves were rolled above his elbows and his tie was loosened, but he still gave no indication of moving on. I simply returned his smile.

"You know, Frank, Jimmy Hanigan's going to get you in a lot of trouble if you let him."

"I'll be sure to watch that. Listen, I've got some work to do here—"

"You really think he's hot stuff, don't you? Fooled you like everybody else around here, hasn't he?"

"Actually, I'd heard you were the hot stuff around here, Bernie." I said this with a surprising amount of menace in my voice, my feet taking me across the room toward him. "Now why don't you go back to whatever it was you were working on, and let me worry about myself?"

"Sure, sure," he answered, raising his hands in front of him with his fingers spread. "But when you get a moment, why don't you ask Jimmy why he's not in law school anymore?"

I put my hand on the door, and would have closed it on him except the fat man was already headed down the hallway.

So that's why Hanigan knows so much about the law. I started going over this new revelation as I went back to the projector, but then made myself stop right there. As the victim of a smear campaign years before, I'd developed a deep disregard for gossip and the people who spread it. Kaplan's reputation in the firm was that of a fact-obsessed courtroom brawler, so I doubted he was actually lying to me, but I felt I'd gotten to know Jimmy at least a little bit by then. Kaplan was an unknown quantity, and I had no intention of letting him pull me into whatever game he was playing.

I turned the projector back on, but it was hard to concentrate. My blood was up, and there was even a moment there when I considered finding the fat attorney and giving him a piece of my mind. I angrily clicked through a couple of the photos until I reached the moment when Pratt blew out the candles.

He'd received some help with that, as his two male grandchildren were blowing air to beat the band on either side of him. The middle son was standing to his grandfather's left, and I could see a man's hand on his shoulder even though it was hard to make out who was standing behind him in the darkness. Someone else was holding the youngest grandchild up in the air, an arm wrapped around the child's midsection. The kid seemed to be having the time of his life, with his head back and one leg thrown out in front of him.

I reviewed the previous photos until I matched the arm to the shirt Neil Graham had been wearing, and then returned to the main event. Since Graham had been holding the youngest Pratt up in the air, the male hand on the other boy's shoulder would have belonged to Thomas. The lights were back on for the next picture, but the cake had been replaced with several wrapped boxes and I decided this one had been taken after the cake-cutting.

I clicked back and forth among the different photos several more times, making brief notes about what I thought was happening, but my heart wasn't in it.

Ask Jimmy why he's not in law school anymore. The words just wouldn't leave my mind.

JIMMY CAME INTO the conference room a short time later. He didn't seem any the worse for wear from his meeting with Walter, but then again it was sometimes hard to tell what Hanigan was thinking.

"Okay, what have you got?" he asked, as if he hadn't just come from the woodshed.

I quickly took him through the photos from the night of the party, and he made an editorial comment or two for Beth Ann's list. He was particularly intrigued by the birthday cake pictures.

"I didn't think of this. They're bringing the cake out, all the lights are off, and then everybody's focused on whether or not he blows out all the candles. Plenty of opportunity to drop something in his drink…which is where?" He was almost talking to himself by then, and walked right up to the image on the screen. "Go back to the first shots of the dinner table. Let's see if we can tell what he was drinking."

Apart from a crystal water glass that was a part of every adult's place setting, it did not appear that Chester Pratt had a beverage at the table. I'd been giving this some thought myself.

"If we're thinking he might have been poisoned, it could have happened earlier. I wonder who was mixing the drinks."

"We'll have to check this, but I gotta doubt that a man in his condition drank much. That doesn't mean he couldn't have been sipping a soda, but I see what you're thinking—it would be easier to drop something in a drink that needed preparing."

I joined him at the screen, which was filled with the image of the Pratt family men gathered around the cake. The light from the candles cast a yellowish glow on their faces, but it seemed to magnify the darkness beyond that. "Are we starting to believe it *was* a poisoning?"

"I'm afraid we have to. A friend of Walter's called to let him know that the preliminary toxicology is back. The autopsy already said this was a heart attack consistent with the drug interaction that almost killed Pratt the first time. The tox test showed the presence of both sets of pills from the baggy, the prescription meds and the sleeping pills. They're almost ready to say that's what killed him."

"That doesn't prove he didn't do it himself. I guess nothing can."

"Nothing except catching whoever did it. That is, if it was a poisoning." He looked at the screen and then reached a hand out to touch the glowing image. "We need to narrow down the list of opportunities, the chances to slip him something, as much as possible before we go asking questions again. Let's go through these pictures one by one to see if Pratt was eating or drinking something different from everybody else. We'll start there."

"And after that?"

"We'll have to ask Belinda if Pratt had a special diet, or if he was the only one drinking coffee that night… things like that. It would be easier to poison him knowing that he was the only one eating a certain part of the meal, or drinking something unusual."

"Even if he wasn't, would the poison have an effect on any of the others if they ate or drank it by accident? This was one drug reacting with another."

"That's true, but this was either a suicide or a murder meant to look like one. If it's a murder, whoever did it wouldn't take the chance that someone else would get sick from those pills, maybe end up at the emergency room getting their stomach contents analyzed. They'd want to make sure that Pratt was the only one who got that dose.

"Besides, this isn't a guaranteed reaction. It's a combination, like you said. If this was a murder, they'd want to make sure the old man got the full amount. They'd try very hard to make sure that happened."

His voice drifted off as he turned his own words over in his head, his index finger gently tracing the ghostly image of the coffee mug.

We called Beth Ann from the office, and learned she didn't need to get the images straight off the camera. This was helpful, because Walter had promised we would return the camera to Lindsay the next day. Beth Ann had a class to teach that night, so we emailed her a file.

It was just as well that Beth Ann wasn't available, because Jimmy had plans for our evening.

"Once the results of that tox test are known, the police are gonna launch a full-scale investigation. We've had some pretty good cooperation from the family so far, but as soon as the cops start reading people their rights, that access is gonna dry up. Different sets of lawyers are going to get involved after that, and we won't be able to learn anything new."

"What if the police still think it was a suicide, and that they'd rather not drag the rich guy's name through the mud?"

"That's exactly why they'll investigate—because he was rich. Throw in the missing will, and they've got motive on everyone at the party except the kids."

"So what's our next move?"

"We're going to watch Lindsay Pratt. I want to see who she meets with when she finds out the cops think this might have been a murder."

"Why her?" Hanigan's impulsive nature had already gotten me in hot water that day, and now it was threatening to throw me right back in the pot.

"Why her? You were there today. She *really* didn't want to hand us that camera. She's got something to hide."

"Did you consider that she might not have wanted strangers coming to her home to take her daughter's stuff? Or that maybe she hadn't looked at the pictures in the camera and was worried just what else an eight-year-old might have photographed in the privacy of their own home?"

"I did, actually. But then I remembered what the police are sure to find out—of the people who didn't like the new will, Thomas and Lindsay Pratt are the only ones who stand to gain from its disappearance."

I MENTIONED EARLIER that I haven't developed a fondness, or even a tolerance, for stakeouts. When I first began working in the investigations business I was little more than a dabbler, doing background checks and retrieving court documents. It was easy, and I made my own hours. I also avoided sitting in the same cramped position in someone else's car or truck for long periods of time, trying to keep focused on a front door that never opened.

Partnering with Jimmy Hanigan had brought me into the world of stakeouts, and I wasn't getting any better at them. Apart from the uncomfortable conditions and the sheer boredom, I'd discovered that I didn't possess the powers of concentration that Jimmy displayed at these times. He could carry on long conversations without once taking his eyes off the target, and he spotted the slightest changes as they occurred. When someone inside passed by a window, or a television set started throwing light onto a drawn curtain, he was always the first to notice.

This didn't stop me from trying to converse with him as we sat outside Thomas Pratt's house that night, however. Even with the afternoon's events fresh in my mind, I still wondered just why he'd zeroed in on Lindsay. In our previous discussions with Walter we'd agreed that everyone named in the will, from the widow to Chester Pratt's children, had stood to gain in some way from that document's disappearance. Belinda would get half the estate even if she said she didn't want it, the Grahams would get their wish to continue their lives independent of Pratt's millions, and Thomas would get a much larger share of the inheritance pie.

That was the part that bothered me most. I could not imagine the man we had met at the restaurant being involved in a murder plot of any kind, much less one where his own father was the target. Lindsay Pratt may have been rude to us, but that did not make her the suspect that Jimmy obviously thought she was. On a more general investigative level, her behavior had done nothing to rule out the others as suspects.

"Jimmy, can you tell me why we're watching the Pratts instead of, say, the Grahams?"

"I thought I already did. Lindsay was acting squirrelly around us, and she stands to gain from the will being lost."

"Belinda stands to gain from the will's disappearance, too. She's getting half of her husband's money if the will is never found."

"She also requested a prenuptial agreement before she married Pratt, and dropped the idea only when he refused to have any part of it. She then forced him to change his will so that the majority of the estate went to Kerry. All she had to do, if she really wanted his money, was leave things alone when she learned that Pratt planned to leave her the bulk of his estate. But she didn't."

"Okay, but what about that moment, newly returned from the hospital, when she was faced with the reality that her husband was dead and most of his wealth was going to a daughter who might not even like her?"

"I could understand that, except getting rid of the

will would mean she'd already have to know how the court would react. That means premeditation. What you're describing is a spur-of-the-moment thing."

"Okay, but what about the fact that Lindsay doesn't have the combination to the safe?"

"Actually, we're only assuming she doesn't. We already established that Kerry wrote the combination down, so who knows if Belinda didn't, too? And what if Lindsay was in the study one time when Chester opened the safe, and looked over his shoulder? There are ways she could find out the combination."

"If that puts the spotlight on her, then why aren't we shining it on Kerry, as well? She's got a house key and the combination, and she was in and out of that safe all the time. She had a ready-made excuse if anyone found her digging around in there, something Lindsay and Thomas wouldn't have."

"Who said anyone was home when the will was taken? Thomas has a key to the house, and he and Lindsay didn't exactly rush to the hospital after they got the phone call. They took their youngest to his grandmother's first. That still strikes me as an odd thing to do. The kid's only three or four, so why not take him along? They knew from the phone call that the house was empty and that Pratt was dead. Saying they had to drop the kid off left plenty of time to go swipe the will."

"That would mean Thomas was involved. You think the guy we met would kill his father? Or, if Pratt wasn't murdered, you think that guy would run over to the house to steal the old man's will?"

"Of course not. I'd bet big money that Thomas has

nothing to do with this. All I'm saying is that Lindsay was in a position to get the key and the combination. She stood to gain from the will's disappearance, and she was very opposed to letting us see those pictures. That's why we're here." He stopped for a moment, and let the edge slide off his voice. "That, and the fact that we caught Barstow staking out the Grahams."

"So you think that means Lindsay or Thomas is paying him?"

"They might be. But that's not what I mean. Bob's not a bad investigator, but when he puts two and two together he usually comes up with five. If he's watching the Grahams, it means they're almost a sure bet to be innocent."

"You sound awfully sure of yourself."

He did look at me just then. "Listen, Frank, we're not ruling anything out just yet. The toxicology only proves that Pratt had the drugs in his system, which leaves plenty of explanations. He may have destroyed the will and then offed himself. Or maybe he killed himself and someone else took the will after that. Or maybe someone poisoned him after taking the will.

"For us, everyone in that will is still a suspect."

THE PRATT NEIGHBORHOOD was a quiet place, and it got a lot quieter after midnight. We'd seen a few kids on bicycles, and the standard late-night vehicle traffic, but very little seemed to be afoot at the Pratt house. Different upstairs lights went off as various children were presumably put to bed, but the living-room light was still visible behind the bay window curtains long after that.

Thomas Pratt came home around one, probably straight from the restaurant. He parked in the driveway, and walked toward the steps looking like a guy who'd had a very long day. The front door opened while he was still on the walkway, and he didn't seem surprised that his wife was waiting for him. They embraced in the light, and were still locked together when the door closed.

That happened during Hanigan's turn to sleep, and I didn't wake him because Thomas Pratt's return didn't seem all that earth-shattering. Now I was glad I'd made that decision, partly because I figured Jimmy would have said something crude about the long embrace at the front door, something about now understanding why the Pratts had so many kids.

But there was more to it than that. I was already close to certain that Thomas Pratt had nothing to do with his father's death or the will's disappearance, regardless of what Hanigan thought. In the final analysis, however, it was the scene at the door, brimming with such simple affection, that told me we were watching the wrong people.

SEVEN

"WAKE UP." I heard Jimmy's voice from across a dark void, and as my eyes opened it didn't get any brighter. It took me a moment, but I remembered crawling into the backseat at roughly two in the morning, and realized I was now staring at the back of the front seat.

I'd been working surveillance long enough to learn two things about sleeping in the back of the car. First, six-footers do not simply sit up after scrunching down into the fetal position for a few hours of exhausted slumber. Second, it is not wise to suddenly pop up when watching someone's house. It's an unusual motion, even when caught out of the corner of the eye, and can attract attention.

So I slowly came up on one elbow, painfully aware of the stiffness in my joints, and looked through the windshield. Hanigan had moved the car while I was asleep, and we were no longer facing the front door. Lindsay Pratt was pulling out of the garage with her two school-age children, and we watched her drive off in the opposite direction.

"Didn't Pratt say he drove the kids to school on the day his father died?" Hanigan asked, scanning the windows for any sign of movement within.

It was full daylight, so I stayed hunched over as I

climbed out of the car and slid into the front seat. "Yeah. He drove the kids to school, and got the phone call just after coming back."

"Interesting. He'd been at his father's birthday party the night before, so maybe when he takes the night off from the restaurant he drives the kids to school the next day. What time did you say he came home last night?"

"Around one." I'd filled him in on developments when he took over watching at two.

Jimmy flipped open his cell phone and spoke to what sounded like one of his many car-loaning friends. He arranged to meet whoever it was just a few blocks away, where we would switch vehicles. I assumed I was in for a long day of tailing Mrs. Pratt when he ended the conversation and proved me wrong.

"Frank, I want you to go back to my place and get cleaned up. Jacket and tie again. Call Emil and have him ask Belinda if you can come out and ask her a few more questions."

"You know, I'm capable of calling her myself."

"Yes, you are. Except I don't know when the toxicology report is going to be released. When that news comes out, sometime today or tomorrow, Belinda's gonna know that her husband was either murdered or committed suicide. We need to be a little careful around her for the time being, so Emil will set this up.

"But we also need to know if she shared the safe's combination with anyone, or wrote it down where a snoop might have found it. That's your assignment for the day. Keep the questions general, don't say anything about who we suspect, but ask Belinda if she ever got the feeling that someone had been in the house when she and Chester were out."

I quickly wrote these items down, thankful that I wouldn't be spending the day stuck in a car waiting for Lindsay Pratt to do something suspicious. As for her, she returned from school just a few minutes later and parked alongside her husband's car in the driveway.

"Looks like Mrs. Pratt intends to go somewhere sometime today," Jimmy observed while turning the key in the ignition. We pulled out quietly, and went to meet whoever was bringing us the new car.

He was waiting when we got there, and climbed out from behind the wheel of a beat-up maroon sedan. He was no more than twenty-five, and still had the thin build of a teenager. A brown T-shirt hung near his ribs, and a large pair of dungarees looked ready to slide down his hips. His hair was brown and shaggy, but he didn't seem put out at having to drop off his car on short notice.

Instead, he gave Hanigan a broad smile and fisted him when he approached, that weird handshake where the young people touch knuckles. They spoke briefly, and even without the sound I could tell that the thin man held Jimmy Hanigan in high regard.

The stranger then walked away as if he hadn't even seen me, which made me wonder how he was going to get anywhere without wheels. Jimmy had borrowed other cars many times during previous surveillance jobs, and we often gave the donor a lift back to his or her place.

"Um, where's he going?" I asked when Hanigan came back.

"Work, probably."

"I mean, how's he going to get there?"

"Bus, probably."

"How's he gonna get his car back?"

"Don't worry about that. We're tight. War buddies, so to speak." Hanigan started walking back toward the sedan, but turned after a few steps. "Remember—kid gloves with Belinda, all right?"

BELINDA PRATT LOOKED like she'd been doing house-work when she greeted me at the door. She also looked like she'd been crying, and I found out why once we had walked into Pratt's study. The boxes were no lon-ger in the center of the room, and most of the books were back on the shelves. Belinda had been putting the room back together again, and it seemed to have had a cathartic effect on her.

"I hope you don't mind if I keep straightening up in here, Frank, but I'd like to get this done." She stopped just short of one of the empty bookcases, with two large volumes in her hands. "We never did find the will."

"But you did accomplish something, just by look-ing," I offered. "You now know it isn't just sitting some-where in here, knocked off a desk by accident. That's something."

"I suppose." She exhaled heavily, and continued reshelving her husband's books. Many of the volumes were large, coffee-table stuff, and I offered to assist but she waved me off. "In a way I think this is helping. I'm putting things back the way Chet had them."

I noted that the door to the safe was closed, and decided to try to edge into the purpose of my visit. "Belinda, we've been trying to piece together any way that someone might have gotten into your husband's safe, and it made me think of something from a job I used to have.

"We worked a lot with computers, and so we had a lot of different passwords for getting on to different systems. People used to write their passwords down and hide them in their desks, because they were concerned they might not be able to remember them when they had to."

"I was like that with Chet's safe." Belinda pointed toward the box. "I didn't go in there much, and I was afraid I'd forget the combination. So I wrote it down."

I smiled at her reassuringly. She didn't seem to notice, instead selecting two more books and walking toward the shelves again, so I continued, "My people used to write the passwords on pieces of paper they kept under their computer keyboards. You could walk through the office and get everything in about five minutes, if you wanted to."

She stopped just then, her fingertips resting on the spine of the last book she'd shelved. When she looked at me, her forehead was a series of ridges. "I kept the combination in my jewelry box upstairs, and also with the emergency numbers in my address book."

"Could you show me the address book?"

She nodded, and led me into the kitchen as if in a trance. A small desk sat off to one side of the large room, and Belinda reached into a cabinet above it. She came down with a well-worn ringed binder covered in blue vinyl, which she set down on the desk.

She opened it to the very first page, and right there, with the helpful notation that this was the combination to Chet's safe, was a series of numbers. She turned to look at me, the tears having found their way back to her eyes.

"Oh, Lord. What did I do?"

WE WERE STILL IN the kitchen a half hour later. It had taken me some time to convince Belinda that there were many ways the will could have disappeared that didn't involve the safe's combination. It wasn't easy to do this without mentioning the chance that her husband had destroyed it before killing himself, but I managed it. We were drinking tea and talking about nothing when the back door opened and Neil Graham walked in.

He was in a dark blue suit, complete with two-tone shirt and cuff links, and he didn't seem happy to see me. He'd come through the door looking normal enough, but it was apparent that Belinda had been crying and I think he got the wrong idea.

"What's going on here? What did you say to her?"

Graham's a pretty big guy, and I'm by no means a street fighter, but my long exile in Florida had topped off the tanks which held my resentment. Guys like him have always rubbed me the wrong way, and I had become less and less inclined to accommodate them the longer I worked in investigations. Hanging around with Jimmy Hanigan had done nothing to reduce this silly machismo, as I discovered while coming to my feet.

"We're just sitting here having a cup of tea, Mr. Graham. I'm looking for the missing will, and that means I'm going to be swinging by from time to time." I dropped the explanatory tone from my voice, trying hard to think what Hanigan would have said next. "Come to think of it, I've been here three times in the last week and this is the first time I've seen you at all."

As if to confirm my assessment of his character, Graham backed off fast. He raised his hands, palm-out and just a little above his waste, while adopting a look of conciliation. In my heat I wondered just how many times he'd practiced that stance on retirees whose nest eggs had declined under his supervision.

"Sorry, sorry," he intoned, actually taking a step backward. "I didn't mean it that way. It's just that, with the bad news, I thought I'd come by, and finding Belinda looking like that…"

I knew what the bad news was, but hadn't been aware that it had reached the Pratt house before me. Now it was my turn to step back, and I sat down uncomfortably.

Belinda had already known the results of the toxicology, then. She'd known that her husband had died from the pills that he had either knowingly or unknowingly ingested. That was why my questions about the safe's combination had hit her so hard. That was why she'd been cleaning up his study and reshelving his library. Almost literally closing the book on her husband's life.

KERRY ARRIVED just a few minutes later, but it was time enough for me to observe Belinda and Graham together. I can't exactly say why, but I quickly came to the conclusion that she disliked him. She hadn't said a word to either of us when we'd had our brief blow-up, and she didn't suggest that I leave once she convinced Graham to sit down.

Kerry came in through the front door and swept Belinda up in her arms as soon as she entered the kitchen. She wore business attire like her husband, and I guessed she'd been at work. Her presence set Belinda to sobbing again, and I watched Kerry exchange looks with her husband over the widow's shoulder. She seemed to be asking if she should take Belinda into the next room, and Graham nodded without making an effort to hide it from me.

These two are very close. They're almost telepathic. The thought came into my mind unbidden, and I wondered if they'd used the same nonverbal communication to handle Chester Pratt when he was alive.

"Tough times here. Tough times," Graham commented once Kerry had led Belinda away. He'd donned a man-of-the-house demeanor now, and I almost told him to save The Many Faces of Neil for the office. But he seemed to want to talk, so I let him go on. "Have you found anything out yet?"

Although Walter had identified Chester Pratt as our client, I considered it pompous to tell the husband of the dead man's daughter that I couldn't discuss the case. I also wanted to ask him a couple of questions, so I left the conversational door open.

"Not a heck of a lot, actually. Of course, now that we have the results of the toxicology report, it suggests that Mr. Pratt may have done away with the document himself." Jimmy Hanigan, it appeared, was not the only investigator at Daley & Associates who could utter a lot of words and reveal almost nothing.

"I'm having some trouble believing Chet killed himself. He had a really good time at the birthday party, and that was just a few hours earlier. He seemed very happy."

I came close to mentioning the photos just then, hoping to see his reaction, but I wasn't sure what the police might think of our having them. They were probably going to start a murder investigation now, and would certainly want to see the photos taken at the party. Of course they could get them from Lindsay, but I had no idea what the status of the firm's copies might be.

"That's what Belinda said. Did you spend much time with him that night?"

"Of course. Between watching the children and getting dinner ready, everybody had a job except me and Chet. He and Thomas seemed to have patched things up about the will, so of course I didn't mention it. Mostly we talked about how my business was going. Chet always wanted to talk about business."

"Really?"

"Oh, yeah. It was in his blood. He sold farm equipment in a lot of places, both here and in Latin America.

Even after he sold the business, he still had investments down there. Lots of travel, lots of interests overseas. Hard to let that go, I imagine."

I had known that Pratt made much of his fortune through investment, but Graham seemed to be suggesting something else here. Overseas business can get pretty unsavory no matter where you do it, and the Panhandle is no exception. There's lots of illicit stuff crossing the Caribbean, and I felt Graham meant for me to make that connection. Even if Chester Pratt had gotten out of the farm equipment field many years before.

I didn't take the bait. "Did he talk at all about the future? A vacation, maybe? The holidays aren't that far off."

"Not that I remember." I made a mental note to ask the other partygoers if Chet had been talking about his plans for Thanksgiving or Christmas. It wouldn't constitute hard evidence that he was in no mood to swallow a bag of pills, but it might help to know if Graham was lying to me. "We didn't talk all that long. As I said before, we weren't best friends."

Kerry called for him from upstairs just then, and he offered to show me out. I declined, saying I knew the way, and then he did something odd. His face took on a helpless smile, and he tilted his head in the direction of Kerry's voice as if to say, "What am I gonna do, the wife is calling." It was the most human thing he'd done since I'd met him, and it so surprised me that I stared at his back until he disappeared into the next room.

That little gesture revealed what had been bothering

me about Neil Graham. I suppose the truth had been lurking somewhere in the back of my mind, because nothing in our conversation had shed any light on this topic. But suddenly I knew.

Graham got on my nerves because he'd stood up to his rich in-laws, but still managed to keep his wife in the process. I had not. My ex-wife's relatives weren't as intrusive as Chester and Caroline Pratt, but then again I doubt I'd ever aroused my in-laws' interest the way Graham had. I remembered them as a petty bunch, engaged in an endless game of one-upmanship with just about everyone they knew, and luckily I didn't have the money to be much sport in that league.

That hadn't kept them from undermining me with my wife in a thousand little ways, or from really turning it on when my business started to fail. It was only after the divorce that I recognized how they'd poisoned Lisa's mind, belittling my efforts to keep my company afloat while simultaneously questioning why I spent so much time at work.

I should have noticed, though, and done something about it. Graham certainly had, and it had worked. He outrightly admitted to disliking Chester Pratt, and seemed sincere in his rejection of the dead man's wealth. While I'd never coveted my in-laws' riches or lifestyle, I had tried very hard to get along with them. Perhaps too hard.

I stood in the kitchen for at least a minute after he left, trying to figure out if I'd alienated the one member of the extended Pratt family with whom I had the most in common.

My cell phone rang as I walked toward my car, and I wasn't surprised to see that it was Jimmy. What was surprising was that he could describe what I was wearing.

"I keep telling you, Frank, but you won't listen. You need to ditch the suits. Get two good jackets, five pairs of pants, and mix and match. The suits really limit your wardrobe."

"Okay, where are you and why are you tailing me instead of Lindsay?" I asked, looking around in the sun. I spotted the maroon sedan from that morning two blocks up the street, and saw Hanigan's arm waving out the window.

"Actually, I'm not tailing you. I'm tailing the guy who's tailing Graham."

"Barstow? He around?"

"Kind of. He followed Graham here, waited until Kerry arrived, and then left. I think he got hungry."

"So how did you end up following Barstow?"

"Because Lindsay met up with him around midmorning. He's obviously working for her, and maybe her husband. It pretty much brought me around to your opinion about those two—I have to figure nobody who'd committed a murder would hire an investigator to look into it.

"There's a burger joint three blocks up the road and two blocks over on the right. Follow me there and we'll talk."

I wondered how Jimmy would know something like that until I saw Bob Barstow seated at one of the sandwich shop's outdoor picnic tables. Hanigan must have tailed the other investigator there from the Pratt house before doubling back to get me. Barstow didn't look to be in a big hurry, so we ordered our lunches and walked over.

"Say hey, Bob. Mind if we join you?" Hanigan asked politely, and then waited for permission to sit. The food stand was near a minor highway, and traffic whipped by just beyond a chain-link fence.

"Suit yourselves. You guys followin' me?" Barstow had shed his jacket, but the brimmed hat still sat on his head. For once he didn't seem in a bad mood.

"Yeah, actually." Jimmy chuckled while saying this, and then set about unwrapping his lunch. "It was an accident, though. I was watching Lindsay Pratt. Seems we're all going to be seeing a lot of each other these next few days."

"I doubt that. I think my part of this thing is going to end pretty soon. Why were you tailing Mrs. Pratt?" If Barstow was upset about being followed, he didn't sound like it.

"You know we're trying to figure out what happened to the old man's will. Near as we can tell, Thomas and Lindsay are the ones who benefit the most from the will disappearing."

Barstow gave a short laugh. "They only get a quarter of the money if the will's never found. The widow gets half, and somehow *they're* the ones making out? If I were you, I'd start watching the dead man's wife."

"Now how would you know the way the estate's gonna get cut up, Bob? Seein' as you're not workin' on what happened to the will."

"I'm not. I didn't lie to you." Barstow took a small bite of what looked like a tuna sandwich, chewing slowly. "Lindsay Pratt told me. She's keeping me updated on what's happening with the rest of the family, seeing as it might affect her ability to pay me."

I began eating my burger, not wanting to do anything to interrupt the rapport which Hanigan had struck up with Barstow. I was surprised that the older investigator hadn't insisted I eat somewhere else, but it suggested that he honestly believed he would soon be finished with his case. Whatever that was.

"Oh, come on, Bob, can we drop the games? Lindsay's got you watching Graham, and there's millions of dollars up for grabs. Now I've got some interesting information for you, and maybe you've got some for me, but can we stop pretending you're not working on the old man's will?"

"I'd love to do that, but it would be a lie. Six weeks ago, Mrs. Pratt hired me to tail Graham for a few days. I didn't see him do anything special, and so she cancelled the job. She called to put me back on just after the old man passed away. That's why you're wrong to suspect Thomas or Lindsay Pratt, just how would they know the guy's will was going to come up missing a month before it happened?"

"She hired you a month before the party? Really?" Jimmy sounded genuinely puzzled. "So what's she got against Graham?"

"Nuthin'. At least nothing I could find. She asked me to tail him, see where he goes and who he meets, and tell her about it. I imagine she thought he was cheating on his wife and wanted to get proof. But from what I saw the guy's clean. I told her the same thing this morning, and I think she's gonna tell me to drop it in the next day or so."

I'd seen cold indifference like Barstow's in other investigators before, and always chalked it up to too many years spent looking through keyholes. Much of the work involves cheating spouses or people fraudulently claiming disability insurance, so it's not a surprise that some P.I.s get a little jaded.

I mentally reviewed what might have caused Lindsay Pratt to sic a P.I. on Neil Graham six weeks earlier, and of course remembered that Chester Pratt had changed his will shortly before that. It probably took Lindsay a while to get good and mad about the new will, and then she hired Barstow to dig up some dirt on the husband of the Pratt who was going to receive the bulk of the estate.

With that conclusion in hand, I came to agree with Jimmy's analysis: Lindsay Pratt would hardly hire a private investigator if she was planning to steal her father-in-law's will. Or help to murder him.

"Thanks for telling me that, Bob. Here's something in return. The toxicology report on Chester Pratt came back, and he definitely swallowed some of the pills found in his desk."

"Yeah, Mrs. Pratt told me he might have taken the same pills that almost finished him a year ago. You think he killed himself?"

"It's possible. And a guy getting ready to kill himself could do just about anything, like burning the will he'd had prepared two months before. But I doubt it."

I was a little surprised to hear Jimmy tossing that much information around with another P.I., and particularly with Barstow, but it wasn't the first unorthodox thing I'd seen him do. Besides, Barstow didn't seem terribly impressed.

"That's good information to have, but it doesn't really relate to what I'm doing."

"Sure it does. I don't think he killed himself, and neither do you. You think it was his wife, which is possible, but it still might have been your client. No matter how the estate's cut up, will or no will, if somebody proves your client killed the guy she gets nothing. You might want to collect your fee right when you present the bill."

"So we've got a will stored in a safe. The combination has been written down in places where just about anybody could find it. The family members had free run of the house, and there were spare keys that could have been duplicated without anyone knowing." Jimmy spoke from memory, seated next to me in front of Walter's desk.

"Chester Pratt had the drugs in his system when he died, and the coroner believes that was what killed him. Two people who stood to gain from getting rid of the will hired Bob Barstow weeks before Pratt's death to watch Neil Graham's comings and goings. They hired Barstow again just after the old man died, with the same assignment."

"We aren't sure if Thomas knows his wife hired

Barstow," I pointed out, following along as best I could from my notes.

"That's right, but it doesn't make much difference in the overall. Right now, the stack of what we don't know is much higher than the stack of what we do know. In effect, we're still dealing with the same possibilities as when we started.

"Maybe Pratt killed himself, and someone took the will after that. Maybe Pratt got rid of it—although it seems unlikely that he'd destroy a will he'd created two months before—and then killed himself. And maybe someone slipped him those pills and then swiped the will."

Jimmy inhaled deeply, exhaled slowly, and then continued, "I thought Lindsay Pratt was a good suspect until we learned she hired Barstow weeks before the murder. Honestly, Walter, at this point I don't know who to suspect."

"Then don't," Walter said calmly. He wore a gray suit today, complete with vest, and seemed untroubled by Jimmy's report. "Basically you've got four things that could have happened here. One, Chet killed himself after destroying the will, for reasons unknown. Two, Chet killed himself and someone took the will after the fact. Three, someone poisoned Chet and took the will. Four, someone poisoned Chet, and someone else took the will after he was found."

"Isn't there a fifth approach? That he died by accident?" I asked that one, and Jimmy responded.

"The bag of pills in the desk says no. Either Pratt

put them in there after swallowing a few, or someone else put them in there so the police would find them."

Walter resumed his instructions. "You have to treat all four scenarios as being possible, and then start applying the facts to each one. Remember, we're trying to find the will—if it's still in existence—or determine who had a chance to destroy it if Chet didn't do it himself. Those are the only two ways we can enforce Chester Pratt's final wishes."

That all sounded neat and tidy, but it didn't seem to point the investigation anywhere. Jimmy seemed to be reading my mind.

"That's kind of what I'm getting at, Walter. They all had access to the house, and they all either knew the combination or could have found it out easily enough. They were all there the night before, and they all stood to gain from the will's disappearance. Belinda gets half the estate, Thomas gets a quarter, and the Grahams get relieved of the responsibility of handling the old man's money."

"While still getting a quarter of the estate," I added quietly.

"Exactly." He turned back to Walter. "Any more word on what the police think happened here?"

"Not yet. Keep working your contacts, and I'll keep working mine. I doubt we're going to get a blow-by-blow of the investigation, but it would help to know which way they were leaning."

Daley's reference to the police jogged my memory just then. "Walter, what's our liability regarding the photos from the birthday party?"

"None that I can see. I'd expect the police to ask for those pictures, but that they'd go to Thomas and Lindsay for them. We've only got electronic copies, and we're not interfering in any way. I suppose if Lindsay erased the photos the police might come to us, but then we'd just give them a copy of the files." His eyes twinkled. "No, your girlfriend's not in any danger, Frank."

"I felt I should ask."

"Darn right. Always ask. Speaking of the pictures, any word from Beth Ann yet?"

"No, she was still blowing the things up, or enhancing them, or whatever it is she does."

"Jimmy, what do you say we cut Frank loose for the rest of the day and give him a chance to go help Beth Ann?"

"Fine by me. He's been on my couch so much the last two weeks my landlord's been asking if I've got a roommate."

"He's probably more surprised you've got a friend." Walter turned to me before Jimmy could respond. "Go on, get out of here. It's a long drive to Bending Palms, or wherever it is you live."

"Exile. I live in Exile."

EIGHT

BETH ANN'S CAMERA STORE was a full-service establishment, with everything from equipment repair to photography classes. Although she plainly preferred the type of camera where you load and develop film, she was conversant in the latest digital equipment, as well. Between her store and the classes she taught at Farragut Community College, it was a wonder she had any time for me at all.

That's why I called ahead to find out if she had eaten yet. I offered to take her out to an early dinner, but she told me to pick up a pizza and some soda instead. I was carrying these items when I rapped on the shop's front door, having arrived shortly after closing time.

"Come in, come in!" she said in a breathless whisper, and I felt like a teenager sneaking in the back door of his girlfriend's house while Dad snoozes in the front room. She took my upper arm in a firm grip, and hustled me through the empty store. We practically raced past displays of lens cleaner and carry cases before arriving outside the door of a darkened room just large enough for two chairs and a large viewing machine of some kind.

"Ooh. I like this spot." I raised the pizza first, and

then the bottle of soda as I recited from *The Rubaiyat of Omar Khayyam*. "'A loaf of bread, a jug of wine—'"

"And thou beside me in a dark, cramped space. Get in here, Omar." I was laughing when I obeyed, but I stopped that when she shut the door behind us. The hall light had obscured the viewing screen, a two-by-three rectangle which now glowed with the image of a man's hand hovering over a white coffee mug. I recognized the tablecloth from the Pratt birthday party.

"Whose hand is that?"

"You'll see in a second. I've been working on this all afternoon." Beth Ann's fingers danced over the keyboard, and the picture was replaced by the original photo. In this one, the flash showed a seated Chester Pratt half turned to look over his right shoulder, while a floating birthday cake hovered in the darkness just behind him.

The youngest Pratt child also seemed to be levitating, leaning out over the table from the shadows on the picture's left side. A man's arm was visible around the kid's waist, and I remembered that Neil Graham had held the child that way when they blew out the candles. The hand I was looking for was reaching around Chester's chair from behind, and the darkness, the flash, and the old man's head blocked the view of its owner.

Not that it mattered. It was a man's hand, which meant it could only belong to Thomas Pratt. I put the pizza and the soda down on a low counter to my right, and whispered to Beth Ann. "Okay."

She hit a key, and an enhanced version of the same picture appeared. It was nothing you'd hang in a museum, but she'd cleaned up the pixels enough to show part of Thomas Pratt's face behind that of his father. He'd leaned over behind Chester's chair to do whatever he'd done with the coffee mug, and was now moving back to his old position, to his father's left.

"Coffee." I exhaled the words. "Jimmy and I talked about this. If you ground the pills into a powder, and had a moment in the darkness to stir it all together, it would be a good way to poison somebody."

"That's what I figured."

"THE MORE I THINK ABOUT this, the better it gets as a scheme." I leaned back in the plastic chair in front of the viewer, my stomach now full. "You wait until the lights are turned out for the birthday cake. You pour the drugs into the coffee in the darkness, and give it a good stir just as the cake is coming out. Lots of noise, everybody looking in the wrong direction.

"The Pratt household is a nice, clean place. So that coffee mug got tossed into the dishwasher that night, hours before the pills took effect. Any residue was washed away. Heck, even if some of the powder fell on the tablecloth, that probably got put in the washing machine right after dinner."

"I've looked at all the other pictures, and I think Pratt's coffee was the only thing he drank that could be used this way. Look here." Beth Ann had enlarged or enhanced many of the key photos from the party, and we had eaten while going over them. She now returned to a photo taken early in the evening, when everyone had been circulating through the house. Chester Pratt could be seen holding a large glass of water, talking to Neil Graham in the living room. "Clear glass, full of water. Unless that's vodka, of course."

"Pratt was a sick man. I confirmed with Belinda that he didn't drink alcohol anymore."

"So that makes it even harder to get hold of his glass. Can you imagine someone offering to freshen up your water?" Despite the gravity of the subject, she giggled just a little.

"Yeah. Mix me a double this time, why don't you?" Sometimes the grisly nature of my work tips me over into a land where lame jokes sound very funny, and I discovered that Beth Ann had already gone there. We both collapsed in helpless laughter for a good thirty seconds. Caught up in the moment, I leaned over to give her a kiss in the darkness. "Great job, honey. Great job."

She pushed me away, still laughing. The light from the viewer caught her eyes, and the challenge they held. "So what's next?"

I HAD TO CALL Jimmy there and then, to let him know what Beth Ann had discovered. I kept telling myself that it wasn't conclusive evidence, and that it simply didn't fit the man I had met, as I dialed. All of that thinking came to nothing once I'd told Jimmy about the picture.

"It sounds like the police are a little ahead of us on this one, ol' buddy." Jimmy had slipped into his Good Old Boy act, and I wondered who he'd been talking to before I called. "The police asked Thomas Pratt to come in for questioning this afternoon, and he's there now."

"Who's representing him?"

"Good question. I think the fur's really gonna start to flying now, 'cause it ain't us. You remember I was wondering why the other family members hadn't lawyered up? Well I guess they were waiting to see what would happen.

"Lindsay called Belinda just after the police contacted Thomas, pitching a real fit. She threatened to tell the police something bad she knows about the Grahams. She hung up before going into detail, but she was with Thomas when he came to the station. You can bet she's spilling whatever she thinks she has."

"What does this do to our investigation?"

"Hard to tell just yet. It's only routine questioning, according to my cop buddy, but if Lindsay has something solid I wouldn't be surprised to see the Grahams signing on a criminal lawyer of their own. One thing's for sure, our nice, cooperative family just turned into a bunch of mutes."

I SPENT FRIDAY NIGHT at my place in Exile, which was important because the mail had begun to stack up. I wouldn't be there all weekend, as I'd accepted an invitation to a Saturday barbecue at the Daleys' long before the Pratt case ever appeared.

I'd been to a couple of these parties since signing on with Daley & Associates, and both occasions had reinforced the image of Walter Daley as chieftain of a sprawling Gaelic clan. Several generations' residence in America might have thinned their Celtic blood, but it didn't stop Walter from feasting various cousins and in-laws every chance he got. He also invited many of the people from work, but that furthered the image of tribal benefactor instead of diminishing it.

I was just finishing a load of laundry at a coin-op in Exile's small town center when my cell phone rang. I thought it would be Beth Ann giving me the final word on her attendance at the Daley's party that afternoon, but it was Hanigan instead.

"We now know why Lindsay Pratt set Barstow on Neil Graham's tail—and it's a lulu. Roughly a year ago, Lindsay happened to see Neil coming out of a motel with a young woman. She kept the information to herself at the time, but when the new will came out she decided to get proof of the relationship. That's why she hired Barstow to tail Graham."

This was a major development, but I saw a glitch in it almost immediately. "I'm sure Lindsay thinks this is bad news for the Grahams, but how does it point the finger of guilt away from Thomas? Graham might be a philanderer, but it doesn't change the fact that he didn't want Pratt's money."

"That's what my cop buddy says. It looks like the police are gonna ask Graham to come in for a little chit-chat, too, but a chance sighting a year ago isn't great evidence of infidelity. The point here is that the accusations are really going to start flying now. If there's any chance at all that the will still exists, this would be the time for whoever took it to try to give it back."

"So the police are investigating…what? If they think Pratt was murdered, they won't care if the will turns up—unless it somehow points to the murderer."

"They're treating this as a homicide, but they haven't

completely ruled out the idea that Pratt killed himself. Right now I think they're fishing. Thomas Pratt was the most likely suspect, so they brought him in. He was allowed to go home after questioning, so who knows if the cops are gonna get anywhere at all with this thing?

"Even so, this may help us out in the long run. If Pratt did kill himself, and the will was stolen by one of the relatives after that, a murder investigation is a powerful inducement for them to return the will."

Something he'd said just then set me off on a different line of reasoning, and I didn't answer right away. The laundry's large dryers were spinning behind me like muffled airplane engines, and I could barely hear Hanigan as he called my name.

"Frank? You still there? Frankie boy?"

"Yeah, yeah, I was just thinking of something. Something you said a while ago. It's not what you see that's important, but what you don't see. Have the police analyzed the pills found in Pratt's desk drawer?"

"Sure, but the pills were exactly what they thought they were. Pratt's prescription medication from his earlier heart attack. What should they have been looking for?"

"I'm sure they were the same kind of pills, but were they leftovers from the batch Belinda threw out? They should check with the pharmacy that filled that original prescription, the one that almost killed him, and see if the pills in his desk were from the same production run."

"I don't see where this leads."

"If the pills in the desk come from the same batch

that Pratt was taking a year and a half ago, then it leads nowhere. But if they're different, then whoever put them there had to buy them, right? That would mean either Chester, or his murderer, bought the pills. New pills. Maybe recently."

"Even if that's the case, it's gonna be very hard to find out where those pills came from, Frank. You can buy this stuff online."

"Not if you were going to use them to end a life. For a murder or a suicide, you'd wanna make sure you got the real McCoy. Something you could rely on. And if Chester Pratt did kill himself, he might have gotten the pills from the same pharmacy that sold him the original batch."

"Okay, I see where you're going. It's a long shot, but if there's a record of Pratt buying more of those pills after they almost killed him, it's proof he meant to do himself in."

"Exactly. He might have gotten them somewhere else, but it's worth checking. Can you nudge your cop buddy to do that?"

"I'd be surprised if they haven't thought of this already, but yeah, I'll suggest it. Good thinking, Frank. You gonna be at Walter's later?"

"Yes. I think Beth Ann's coming, too, so I'll ask her to bring the photos from the party. Maybe the three of us will see something other than Thomas Pratt's hand."

Hanigan replied in mock seriousness. "It's not what you see. It's what you don't."

We both laughed, and I hung up.

WALTER DALEY'S PLACE sat by a large lake a few miles southwest of Tallahassee, so it wasn't quite as long a drive as the normal run from Exile to the capital. The side roads leading to Walter's place were hard-packed tan dirt surrounded by woods. The trees were a wild mix which alternated mostly between pine and palm. Many of the palm trees sported the out-jutting stubs of previous generations' growth in the center of otherwise smooth trunks, and I had always likened them to pine cones. I'm sure someone could explain what those protuberances were, and why some of the palms had them while others did not, but I called them pine cone palms.

The area was prone to brush fires, and you couldn't ride very far down those country roads without seeing at least one spot where the rolling ground hadn't been blackened by flame. The undergrowth in those spots would of course be gone, but most of the scorched areas were so small in size that the fires that created them probably burned themselves out. Tall pines with green branches still stood in those places despite their darkened lower trunks, and I remembered that the region was home to a hardy species of pine resistant to both fire and insects.

Embankments of red clay flanked other sections of the road, and some of these sported washouts which had then been baked hard by the sun. Viewed as a whole, the ground and vegetation gave an impression of a feral kingdom where nature still did pretty much whatever it liked.

The Daley house gave off a similar vibe of wild growth. I'd been there twice before, and wasn't surprised to see a large number of people scattered across the lawn when I drove up with Beth Ann. It was still hot enough for swimming, and several children could be heard frolicking in the Daley's inground pool.

The building itself was a sprawling, beige conglomeration of railings, gabled windows and even a round tower with a conical roof. Walter might wear a three-piece suit to work, but I think he wanted to make sure his home was a place where people actually lived. Beach towels, bicycles and athletic equipment were strewn along the side porches, and other indications of the many Daley children could be seen on the lawn.

The Daleys' long, curving driveway was paved, but the parking area was gravel. I stopped next to an eclectic assortment of guest vehicles ranging from expensive cars to pickup trucks, many of which had out-of-state license plates. Beth Ann had been there with me before, and we were greeted by Walter's wife as we came around the side of the building.

Deidre Daley was a laughing-eyed redhead who managed the unruly Daley brood with consummate ease. Her people were Scots-Irish from low-country South Carolina, and she made great sport of Daley's obsession with his Gaelic heritage.

"Frank! Beth Ann! How good of you to come!" She gave each of us a big hug, and then pressed us together shoulder-to-shoulder so she could make her usual observation. "What a beautiful couple. You two were made for each other."

Walter rescued us just then, halfheartedly racing one of his younger children for a soccer ball that had been kicked around the corner. It was hard to keep track of the Daley offspring, so I only managed to identify the child as a boy before he ran off with the ball. Walter came up then, wiping a hand on a large green apron which sported a golden map of Ireland.

"Frank! Good to see you. Jimmy's already here." He looked back over his shoulder toward the lake. "Somewhere, anyway. I just fired up the grill, so make yourselves at home. There's beer in the fridge inside, you know where everything is."

He lunged suddenly, catching Deidre around the waist and planting a kiss on her cheek. She laughingly tried to slap him away, and he spoke to us while wrestling with her. "Run for it while you have the chance! She'll have you two married before dinner if you're not careful."

Looking at Beth Ann, I had to admit that wasn't such a daunting prospect. She was fond of sleeveless tops, and today she wore one that was sky-blue with white buttons down the front. She had on a set of white shorts that showed off her legs, and she'd let her hair hang freely, as well. It was usually done up in a ponytail, and I told myself she was wearing it loose because she knew I preferred it that way. She took my hand as we walked.

Coming around the corner, we were faced by at least a dozen adult faces, and quite a few children. I recognized Bernie Kaplan, trying to hide his girth under a red guayabera, which hung over a set of tan trousers. His wife, a warm, dark-haired lady whose name I usually couldn't recall, stood next to him in a white pantsuit which showed her figure to advantage. She was watching their two children splashing around with the swimmers, and Bernie was talking to one of Walter's many relatives. Patches of red hair in the gathering suggested that some of Deidre Daley's low-country relatives were present, but that was as much as I could tell about the other guests.

A strong pair of arms wrapped around me from behind, lifting me off the ground for just an instant, and I knew that I had finally located Jimmy Hanigan.

"I'm gonna throw you in the lake!" he shouted, but by then my feet were back on the grass and he groaned in fake exertion. "And maybe not!"

Mandy, wearing a black summer dress dappled with red, stepped up to Beth Ann while I struggled with her boyfriend. "Come on, Beth Ann. Let the boys play a while. Maybe it'll tire them out."

THE DINNER MENU spanned the gamut from hot dogs and hamburgers to crab cakes and a shrimp gumbo that was a meal in itself. It was also a whirlwind of conversation, much of it shouted, and when it was all done I found myself sitting inside with Beth Ann. We had found a secluded spot that happened to be the Daley formal dining room, and had taken our coffees in there for some peace and quiet.

That didn't last long, though, as Hanigan soon came in talking on his cell phone. He stopped when he saw us, ended the conversation, and then shut the phone. "Glad I found you two. That was my cop buddy, and he said they just got done talking to Neil Graham. They asked him about the strange woman that Lindsay saw him with, and he said he had no idea what she was talking about."

"Not surprising," Beth Ann commented while giving me a friendly kick under the table. "Men."

"Yeah, but there's more." He looked at me for this one. "This relates to that question you had earlier, Frank. The cops already knew that the pills in Pratt's desk weren't from the same batch as the ones that almost killed him earlier. They liked your idea about seeing if Pratt might have bought them, so they went to visit his pharmacy.

"The folks behind the counter knew Pratt pretty well, at least well enough to be sure they didn't sell him the pills that were found in his desk. They said that medication is still on the market across the country, with the appropriate drug interaction warning, so Pratt could have gotten them somewhere else."

"Why do they think he did it at all?" Beth Ann seemed deeply puzzled. "Don't we have a picture of his son monkeying around with his coffee mug?"

"Good question. The police asked Thomas about that, and he insisted he was only moving the mug out of the way so Belinda could put the cake down. The detectives called Belinda, and she said she remembered seeing him do that. Even if she hadn't, there's no way of knowing whether or not the pills were in the coffee at all."

"So you're going to just assume the poor man killed himself."

"I didn't say that." Jimmy sounded almost hurt,

but he deflected the accusation by dropping it on me. "Frank, have you done something to upset Beth Ann?"

"Upset her? We were having a nice cup of coffee here, before you walked in."

Hanigan looked around then, as if recognizing his surroundings for the first time. "Coffee, huh? On a large rectangular table. Just like the Pratts'."

"Aw, come on." I'd been enjoying the quiet interlude with my girlfriend, and wished Hanigan hadn't found us. "Can't we let work go for the evening?"

"No, he's right." Beth Ann stood up and took a step back from the table. "I'm surprised I didn't notice this before. This room is almost identical to the one in those photos. Do you think the Daleys have a highchair?"

OF COURSE THIS WAS my fault, because I'd asked Beth Ann to bring the photos along and we couldn't have re-created the birthday scene without them. She'd enlarged all of the pictures taken when the lights were out, and mounted each of them on a hard backing, which allowed us to stand them up on various pieces of furniture around the room.

The photo showing Thomas's hand withdrawing from his father's coffee mug stood off to the side on a low bureau that probably held the Daley family silver. The shot of Pratt blowing out the candles sat on the arms of a chair placed at the head of the dinner table, and another picture of the male partygoers getting in position around the cake was set up on a windowsill.

The three of us stood at the opposite end of the table and gave the candle-blowing scene a good long stare before deciding we weren't seeing anything new. We got lucky just then, as Mandy came through looking for Jimmy and we hijacked her fresh set of eyes.

"I'm really not sure how much help I can be here," she protested as Jimmy guided her across the room. She seemed to recognize the scene almost immediately, however. "Oh, this isn't that awful case you're working on, is it? The one where the man was poisoned?"

I logged that little tidbit away for the next time Jimmy tried to bust me for telling Beth Ann about a case, but Hanigan was in full persuasive swing.

"Listen, you're a contemporary art student, and you work in a gallery. Who's going to notice fine detail better than you?"

She gave him a halfhearted look of exasperation, and then focused on the job. The shadows were getting long on the lawn outside, so we flipped on the lights. Mandy folded her arms in front of her and stood stock still, and for some reason the rest of us stopped moving, as well. Deidre Daley's voice could be heard clearly from the kitchen, where she and "the womenfolk," to use her term, were cleaning the dishes.

"You think something was dropped in the man's coffee when the lights were out. Right?"

"That's what we're thinking, yes."

"The tall guy holding the youngest child is on the side with the coffee mug. That would put him in a good position to do something, wouldn't it?" She indicated Neil Graham, on Pratt's right in the middle picture.

"Yes, it would," Jimmy murmured, moving a little

closer to the image but still keeping himself out of Mandy's line of sight. "What else do you see?"

"He looks phony to me. If this were a posed photo, I wouldn't believe the model playing him. The kids are both having fun, the old man and the other guy are laughing, but the tall one looks like he really wishes he wasn't even there."

"He may have. He didn't like his father-in-law." Jimmy was now staring at the photo, his hand on his chin. I answered him, more for Mandy's benefit than his.

"That's true, but Belinda said everyone was getting along. And Graham's helping Thomas's youngest to blow out the candles. Going off of the other pictures, Graham was right here, but the kid he's holding was sitting in the high chair over there. He'd have to go all the way around the table to get him, which I'd take as a sign he was trying to help out."

"You ever see kids at a birthday party, Frank?" Beth Ann asked gently. "I bet he climbed down and ran around right next to grandpa as soon as they told him he was going to help blow out the candles."

"Let's see." Jimmy replaced the candle-blowing picture with the shot just before it, the one where Belinda was bringing out the cake and Thomas's hand was near the coffee mug. Neil Graham stood off to the side, out of the way on Chester Pratt's right, holding the youngest Pratt in front of him. "No way to tell if he went over and got him, or if the kid came over himself. But we could always ask."

"Ask who?" Walter's voice came from the door leading into the back of the house. He came into the room with a cheery smile, but that vanished as soon as he saw the photos. He shifted his eyes from the one at the head of the table to the one on the bureau and then the one on the windowsill, and began shaking his head sternly. "No, no, no."

I thought we were about to be served a mighty helping of "things we don't discuss with strangers," but I was wrong. Walter stepped a little farther into the room, his right hand held up and out, as if he were sticking his spread fingers into an imaginary waterfall.

"You've got a dining room, a big table, pictures of the scene and a yard full of adults and small children, and yet you're content to just use the pictures. Your jury would never be able to follow you." He plucked the center photo off of the chair and set it up next to the one on the bureau. "Frank, you stand here in Graham's spot, Jimmy you play Thomas, and—

"Bernie!" He called out the open window, even though the corpulent attorney was nowhere to be seen. "I want Bernie to look at this. He's done reenactments like this in court before."

"Oh, come on, Walter," Jimmy protested petulantly.

"Give the feud a rest for a night, willya, Jim?" Walter said this evenly, but it was clear he was tired of his battling subordinates. "Ten years from now, you two will be the firm's hottest lawyers—and you'll be best friends, too. Seen it a hundred times."

"Don't count on a hundred and one."

Bernie walked in then, looking unsurprised to have been summoned to this odd scene. He took it all in for a moment, and then began nodding his head. "Like the pictures. Who did 'em?"

"I did. I'm Beth Ann, we were introduced earlier."

"Beth Ann Thibedault. I remember. Great job with the photos. You enhanced them?"

"Yeah, took forever. The lighting was terrible."

"Bernie, the lighting's one reason we're focusing on these scenes in particular. If someone poisoned Chester Pratt, it might have happened when the lights were off for the birthday cake."

Bernie pointed at the coffee mug in the pictures on the bureau. "Coffee cup's a good vehicle. Conceals the taste, you could stir it up a little even…and then it goes in the dishwasher."

He looked at Walter. "I'm liking this scenario a lot. Let's see. Two kids, say four and six. I think we've got a couple of those outside."

I'D NEVER SEEN the Daley & Associates team click into action before, and certainly not in the owner's dining room. Mandy and Beth Ann's presence didn't seem to bother the lawyers, but they did shut the doors and windows once Bernie had selected two children from the now-tiring pack on the back lawn. They were amazingly docile, and made more so by an ice-cream bar apiece.

Mandy had been asked to play the role of Belinda Pratt, carrying a cake platter similar to the one in the pictures. One of the younger lawyers had been asked to sit in for Chester Pratt, which put him between me and Jimmy and the two borrowed youngsters. Walter and Bernie put us through so many reenactments that my arms began to ache from lifting a small child into the air.

"Hold Jerry a little higher, Frank," Walter directed, as if sensing my fatigue. He pointed at the coffee mug, which was now off to my right. "See how far away Thomas moved that? And he did it with Graham standing close by and Belinda coming into the room. If he wanted to use the cover of darkness, I think he'd have done it a lot sooner."

"But in that picture he was only moving the thing, and you say that's confirmed by Belinda." Bernie stood next to Walter, his arms folded as he mused. "Maybe he dropped something in it when the lights were first turned out and people's eyes were adjusting. Frank, go back to where Graham was standing before the cake came in."

I carried not-so-little Jerry Kaplan off to the bureau side of the table. In the picture where Thomas's hand was near the coffee mug, Graham was standing not two feet away with Thomas's youngest son held in the air in front of him.

Beth Ann had brought along smaller printouts of the other pictures from the party, and these were strewn about the end of the table where Walter, Bernie and Beth Ann stood. Walter picked one up, examined it, and then held it up for the other two.

"See this? The photo before the lights were turned off? The coffee mug is just off to the right of Chet's place setting. I think it would be a very awkward thing for Thomas to reach around behind his dad and drop something in there."

"And if he did, why did he move the mug afterward? Why attract suspicion?" Beth Ann joined in.

"Maybe he had the pills or the powder in his hand, and he dropped it in while pretending to move the mug." Bernie squeezed his considerable belly down the other side of the table, and then between the spot where Hanigan and one of the Daley children pretended to be Thomas Pratt and son. He reached around behind the befuddled firm lawyer playing Chester Pratt, and moved the coffee mug with his fingers spread over its mouth. "See? He could drop it in like that, and nobody would be the wiser."

"I suppose that could work, but I don't see him doing it that way. This was a heavy overdose, of two kinds of pills," Walter commented judiciously. "Just dropping them in there would be taking a big chance they wouldn't all dissolve. You'd want this all ground up in a powder, which would be hard to handle the way you're holding that cup. And I still think you'd want a chance to stir it in."

Bernie straightened up, obviously thinking, while Jimmy glowered at him from behind. Mandy, standing near the door on our side of the table, took the opportunity to set down the cake plate and step up.

"Why are you thinking it happened here at all? If you really wanted to make sure the pills, or the powder, or whatever it was dissolved, wouldn't you just make sure you mixed his coffee yourself?" She looked around at a suddenly silent room. "I mean, that's how I'd do it. Isn't that how you'd do it?"

"You know, I just assumed that somebody putting poison in that man's coffee wouldn't want a direct connection to it. Like fixing the coffee in the first place." I shook my head at Jimmy as he drove us down a darkened suburban street not far from Thomas Pratt's house.

As I had feared, the reenactment had convinced Jimmy that it was time for another visit to the Pratts. He'd become increasingly annoyed by Bernie's involvement in the process, and this had left him fixated on the last idea in his head before Walter had entered the dining room. Although it was late, he wanted to find out just how the youngest Pratt child had migrated to the other side of the dinner table before the birthday cake had been brought out.

"Told you Mandy was smart. She comes up with things I'd never dream up." He paused, his lips puckering for a moment. "Although I have to think that Belinda fixed Pratt's coffee…so maybe it's not that good a question after all."

"Isn't it?"

"How many times do we have to tell you this, Frank? Belinda didn't do it."

"Why not consider it? Because she made some noises about wanting a prenup? Because she made her husband set up a will she knew she could destroy whenever she wanted to?"

"Are you saying that was a smoke screen? To get half her husband's money? She'd have gotten *all of it* if she'd just kept her mouth shut about the original will. And she obviously wasn't gonna have to wait long, either. No. That doesn't make any sense."

"So what we're doing does make sense? Knocking on the door of the dead man's son, after he's been questioned by the police and gotten himself a lawyer?"

Jimmy gave me an impish smile that was caught for one frozen second by a streetlight as we passed. "Who says we knew he retained counsel?"

I still had fresh memories of our earlier reception on the Pratt doorstep, but Jimmy beat me to the punch.

"Look. We both agree that he's not the type. It was his *father,* for God's sake. And his wife hired a P.I. to sniff around both before *and after* her father-in-law's death. Not exactly the act of someone who was plotting a crime.

"And that's how we're going to approach them. We have to convince them we're on their side, that we're trying to get to the bottom of this, and that we need their help."

"Even if they buy it, they're not going to wake the kids for us."

"You let old Uncle Jimmy work that one. Right now I need you to start thinking of all the different questions we have to ask here, because something tells me we're only going to get the one chance." He snorted briefly, having thought of something funny. "But you're right about one thing—the phones at Daley & Associates are gonna be ringing off the hooks once the Pratts' new lawyer finds out we were here."

He'd shut off the headlights by then, as we were coming down the side street which faced the front door.

Lights still burned in the house, but someone had drawn the shades on the big bay window. There was no movement inside that I could detect, but Jimmy wasn't willing to wait. I followed him out of the car, and we crossed the street quickly.

My heart was pounding when we rang the bell. I was having visions of Lindsay Pratt screaming for her husband to call the police, followed by images of flashing lights and handcuffs, when the door opened. What I saw in that doorway, in that frozen instant of time, suddenly made arrest look like a very rosy way to spend the rest of the night.

Thomas Pratt, wearing a dress shirt unbuttoned over a dark pair of trousers, greeted us with a bottle of whiskey in one hand and a large black revolver in the other. His eyes were wild, and he appeared to have been crying. He didn't remember us at first, but that might have been better than what happened when he did.

"Well, hello!" he muttered in a throaty, low voice, which scared me much more than if he had shouted. "Looks like my good friends from my Pop's law firm. The guys who were only trying to help.

"Well have a look!" he raised his voice only slightly as he waved the bottle behind him. We could only see down a short hallway from where we were standing, but that didn't seem to matter. "Yep, the place is empty! Ya wanna know why?

"So my kids wouldn't have to see their daddy getting arrested. That's right! I sent 'em away with my wife. Can you beat that? The cops think I killed *my own father,* and that means I have to send my own family away."

He stopped himself then, and took a lurching step deeper into the hall before beckoning with the gun. "But where are my manners? Come in, come in, *do* come in! Heck, you invited yourselves here the other day, so why not come in?"

He was backing away now, a bit more certain in his footing, and the gun was pointed right at us. I honestly expected Jimmy to tell him we wouldn't be joining him, so it was a bit of a surprise when he walked past me. I was downright shocked when I followed, looking at my feet and wondering why they were moving. And you could have knocked me over with a feather when I reached out and shut the door behind us.

NINE

"So HERE's WHAT I think, I think you two only half listened to me the other day. I think you picked what you wanted to hear, and left out the part about Pop telling me my family would be taken care of. And I bet you told the police that the only member of the whole family who didn't like the will was little brother Thomas.

"Pretty close, huh?"

Thomas Pratt paced in front of us, his shirttail swinging back and forth with his swaying form. He'd told us to sit on the couch, and so Jimmy and I had complied. Hanigan hadn't said a word yet, and I could only imagine he believed Pratt wasn't going to shoot. He didn't look like he was getting ready to lunge at the guy, which was good because the couch was far too broken in to provide much of a launch platform. Pratt was five feet away, and anyone pushing off of that sofa was probably going to get shot before covering a yard.

"Mr. Pratt, we're here because we know you're innocent." Jimmy finally spoke, his words low and soothing. It was the first time I ever actively rooted for Hanigan's chameleon act.

"Gosh, that's nice." Pratt smiled with a silly, eye-batting expression on his face. "Tell me something.

Sitting here with a gun on you, would you be likely to say anything different from that?"

"Mr. Pratt, did you know the police questioned Neil Graham today? After letting you go? No one's coming to arrest you."

"Same question. I'm pointing a gun at you. What would I expect you to say?" Pratt actually stumbled for a moment, having caught the tip of his shoe on the carpet. That made him stop pacing, and brought his eyes back on to the sofa.

He stood there glaring at us, the weapon steady, and I got the feeling he was coming to a decision. He did, too, because he started pacing again. "So here's what's gonna happen. You two are gonna *listen* this time. You're gonna hear me say the words I had to say at the station today." He stopped suddenly, and shouted for the first time.

"I did not kill my Pop! I did not kill my own father!" He waved the pistol for emphasis, and unfortunately when he stopped doing that the gun was aimed right between my eyes. A strange thought entered my mind as I sat there motionless: *Why's he pointing the gun at me? It wasn't my idea to come here.*

I guess he never meant to shoot me, because he stepped away just then and even turned his back on us. He staggered toward a set of latticed glass doors, which stood open before a carpeted hallway. The gun was at his side as he walked, muttering over and over again that he didn't do it.

"Mr. Pratt?" Jimmy said, the soothing tone gone now. He still sounded like a cop trying to talk someone down off a ledge, but a cop who has decided to stop negotiating. "Look down, Mr. Pratt."

We both obeyed him, and I finally learned why Jimmy Hanigan always wore those silly boots. I'd been working with him for months, and had frequently heard him propound on the evils of handguns, and so I was both thunderstruck and overjoyed to see that he'd been packing the entire time.

The black pistol he held was one of the smallest I've ever seen, and it looked as slim as a Zippo lighter. His right pant leg was now wrinkled above the top of the boot, where a flap of leather stood out. The pistol had probably been concealed there for as long as I'd known him, but the emotion I felt at that instant was pure relief. I actually sagged when I saw the thing.

I didn't stay relaxed for long, though, because the room filled with an explosion a moment later. I'd once had a pistol fired only inches away from my unprotected ears while I wrestled with the weapon's owner, but this gunshot was so unexpected that I actually jumped up in fright.

Or maybe it was because the man sitting next to me on the sofa had just been shot. Pratt had swung his weapon up wildly just before the report boomed in the small space, and Hanigan had jackknifed forward as if his stomach had been split in half. For all I knew, it had.

Pratt and I both stood there for what seemed like a long time, and it was hard to say who was more surprised. The bottle fell out of his hand while his mouth formed an oval, and then a complete circle. His face contorted into an expression of total dismay, and the revolver followed the bottle to the carpet.

Hanigan, doubled over and clutching his left side near the hip, slowly slid forward until his backside landed on the floor with a plop. I think my mouth was hanging open by then, too, but in following his short trip to the carpet my eyes fell on the slim black pocket gun. He'd dropped it when Pratt's bullet hit him.

Pratt took a step backward, and then threw a quick, frenzied look behind him as if gauging the distance to the glass doors. A lot of different ideas were flying through my head in that moment, most of which involved getting Jimmy to a doctor, but something else welled up behind them when Pratt took that look over his shoulder. I was going to need help with Hanigan, and the only available assistance was getting ready to sprint out the back door. A bitter-tasting, jaw-clenching anger surged up into my head, and I dropped to one knee without giving it a moment's thought.

He knew what I was about to do, and he took another step backward as I reached down and snatched up Hanigan's fallen weapon. Beth Ann had introduced me to firearms early in our relationship, and to my surprise I'd turned out to be a pretty good shot. I brought the pistol up, fighting to work my finger through the tiny guard.

"Hold it right there, Pratt!" the words came out in a bellow, and I think that was what made him run. One instant he was standing there shaking his head, his mouth still open, and the next he was all flying shirttail.

I honestly meant to shoot the wall next to the glass

doors. I meant to scare him, and squeezed the tiny trigger expecting, at the worst, to see a shower of glass fragments if I missed. But nothing happened.

Nothing happened. The trigger didn't even move. I jerked my hand down, opening my palm to see if there was some sort of safety on the thing, but of course Pratt was already gone by then. Enraged even further by this crazy development, I tossed the silly popgun onto the sofa and reached out for Jimmy.

"Get something to use to stop the bleeding, okay?" he whispered, and for the first time I saw the blood. He'd been hit low in the abdomen on his left side, and his shirt and trousers were rapidly turning a dark red. He had both hands pressed on the wound, but it didn't seem to be doing any good.

I ran through the glass doors the way Pratt had gone, looking for the kitchen. Luckily I ran in the wrong direction, because I found myself in the Pratts' bedroom instead. I didn't have much time to take in the furnishings, but I did have the presence of mind to snatch up a dark blue terrycloth bathrobe that was tossed on the bed. I ran back into the living room to find Hanigan in the fetal position, breathing heavily.

"Here, here," I said, raising him up into a sitting position so that he leaned back against my chest. I was just about to press the bathrobe onto the blood when he stopped me.

"Wait. Look at my back. Any blood there? Look for an exit wound." His voice was thick, as if he was choking.

I did as he instructed, and was relieved to see that there was nothing. "No, it's clean. What do I do now?"

He leaned back against my chest, and gave me a weak smile. "What do you do now? Who taught you first aid?"

"Um...nobody."

"First rule." He lifted a red hand from his waist and took a corner of the bathrobe, reciting between gasps as he began packing the material under his other hand. "Lie. Tell the patient he's gonna be fine. No matter what you see."

I started helping him, bundling up the thick cloth so we could get more pressure. It seemed to be stanching the flow, but then again it might have just been soaking it up. I was focused on getting more of the bathrobe under his hands when he looked up, his face pale.

"Frank. Get my cell phone. Hit the speed dial. Button number two."

"Who's that? Ambulance?" I found the phone and opened it up.

"Yep. Buddies of mine. We're at 95 Hillcrest. Tell 'em Jimmy H has been shot."

I brought the phone up with one hand, reaching down with the other one to add my weight where Hanigan was clutching the robe. A male voice answered on the second ring, and I told him what had happened and where we were. He shouted a one-syllable swear word, assured me they would be there in moments, and then was gone.

"You get 'em, Frank?" Hanigan's voice was fading, and his head lolled back onto my shoulder. I stuffed the cell phone in my pocket, took him in both arms and pressed down on the wound as hard as I could. He gave a small yelp then, and spoke once more before lapsing into silence. "How's it look, Frankie?"

"It looks fine, Jimmy. It's fine. You're gonna be fine."

WHEN THE PARAMEDICS got there, I thought they were the police. I had my reasons for this error. First, they roared up so close to the house that I thought they'd driven across the lawn. It turned out they had, and so the flashing lights from their rig came through the front curtains like a laser light show seen through a fog bank. At least they'd killed the siren.

Next, they kicked the front door open, and when the first one burst into the living room he was armed. I'm still not sure what part of Tallahassee they served, but I suspect their supervisors would not have been pleased to see the hardware. It wasn't until much later that I realized any ambulance on Jimmy Hanigan's speed dial was unlikely to be the standard meat wagon.

There were two of them, and they came at me from different directions. The older one was in his forties, with graying blond hair that hung over his ears and a walrus mustache. He was wearing a short-sleeved white shirt and blue uniform pants, but what really got my attention was the handgun he was pointing at the floor near my feet. It was the largest revolver I have ever seen, and if intimidation was the desired effect it succeeded admirably with me.

"Your hands! Show me your hands!" he shouted while a younger medic in roughly the same getup came at me through the glass doors, which Pratt had used for his escape. The younger one held a smaller pistol, but I had had quite enough gunplay for the evening, regardless of the size of the weapons.

"I'm Frank Cole! I'm his partner! And I'm not showing you my hands!" I shouted at the older one. "He's *shot,* get it? Now come over and help me!"

"The gun! Where's the gun!" he yelled back, but the younger one spotted Pratt's pistol and answered for me.

"It's over here." They seemed to know their way around crime scenes, because instead of picking the thing up, the younger medic kicked it under a small couch near the glass doors. I had no idea where Jimmy's pistol had ended up, and was no longer in a cooperative mood, so I didn't tell them about it.

The younger one came up then, after stuffing his handgun in the back of his trousers. He wore a blue windbreaker over his white shirt, and it hid the gun from view. He crouched down and felt for a pulse in Jimmy's neck, still talking. "Sorry, buddy, ya never know what you're getting into when there's been a shooting. Better safe than sorry, right?"

The older one had disappeared by then, and I could only guess that he'd gone to get the medical equipment now that the firing range was closed for the night. The younger man, who sported a full head of curly brown hair, now found something that obviously pleased him. He brightened up considerably, and shouted toward the shattered door.

"Hey, Charlie! The stupid Mick's still alive! Chop chop, buddy, we gotta move him right now!"

SOMEONE ONCE TOLD ME that friends and family no longer ride in ambulances with the sick or injured, but this was yet another rule flaunted by Hanigan's friends. They told me that I would be needed in back, and that turned out to be true once the truck got moving.

Charlie, the medic with the mustache, drove as if he'd earn a bonus for making the machine roll over. The other one, who I would later learn was named Bert, replaced the bathrobe with a sterile dressing. He told me to put pressure on it, even though my arms were absolutely killing me by then, and proceeded to stick some kind of IV needle in Jimmy's arm. Considering the heavy turbulence caused by the driver, I have to give the kid credit for hitting the vein on the first try.

As things turned out, their radical approach to first aid was exactly right. Jimmy had lost a lot of blood and they had no idea where the bullet had gone inside him, so getting him to a doctor as fast as possible was the only answer. We screeched up under the Emergency Room awning of a large hospital, and I ran alongside Jimmy's gurney until a pint-size nurse in surgical scrubs hip-checked me out of the way.

Jimmy disappeared into a brightly lit room jammed with official-looking machines and even more people in scrubs, and the doors swung shut behind him. It had all happened so fast that I suddenly found myself alone in the hallway with no idea of what to do. I simply stood there, aching arms hanging in front of me, until the two medics came back. I honestly have no idea how long they were in there.

Charlie clapped me on the back, a big smile visible

under the walrus hair. "Good job there, buddy! I think you saved his life."

"Is he gonna be all right?"

"How should I know? Am I a doctor?" His face was wrinkled in mirth, and I started to catch on that this was how these two cowboys dealt with their job. Seeing my blank reaction, he decided to let up on the act. "Seriously, I've carted a lot of gunshot cases in here, and everything I saw is good. We got him here in record time, and the docs have him now. I'd put money on him being just fine."

"What are they doing?"

"The bullet's still inside, so they gotta go get it. Beers and bullets. You don't buy 'em. You just rent 'em."

"Hey, Charlie." Bert made a gesture toward my midsection, and I noticed for the first time that I looked like I worked at a butcher shop that was running short of aprons. I started wiping at it absently, so the two of them took me by the arms and started walking me toward the stairwell.

"Let's get you cleaned up here, buddy. There's a shower in the janitors' locker room that they let us use in moments like these. We can loan you a shirt, but you're gonna have to call somebody for the rest. What did you say your name was?"

"Frank. Frank Cole. I work with Jimmy."

Once we were in the locker room, the younger one checked the stalls to make sure we were alone. One of the overhead lights flickered an annoying semaphore, and I could hear water dripping in the shower. Charlie was helping me out of my shirt when Bert came back. He held out his hand, palm up, and I saw he was holding Hanigan's tiny automatic. He must have scooped it up back at the house.

"Is this Hanigan's?"

I nodded while Charlie handed me a large towel, which I wrapped around me. The other medic sniffed at the pistol.

"This thing hasn't been fired, right? Try to remember—it's important."

"No. I tried, but I think the safety's on."

The two of them shared a small laugh at that, and Bert retracted the slide just enough to look into the chamber.

"No such thing as a safety on one of these, Frank. But you do have to put one in the chamber before it'll fire." He slid the thing into his pants pocket. "Lucky you. If you'd cranked one off back there, the cops would know there was a second gun in the room.

"I'm gonna keep this until the wild man is back on his feet, okay? Tell the cops about it, and it goes in the lake." He smiled at me just before Charlie guided me to the sink to wash my hands. "But believe me, Frank, you don't wanna even mention this little number to the police. Ya didn't shoot it, so what difference does it make? It wasn't there. Okay?"

My mind was still in a fog, but I had to ask just how these two were so familiar with Jimmy Hanigan, and so concerned with his reputation. "How do you guys know Jimmy?"

"Who doesn't?" The younger one laughed once, but then explained, "Jimmy H and I played football together in high school. And of course we bump into each other from time to time on the job, if you know what I mean."

I took a long time showering, but they were still there when I came back out. That was good, because I probably would have wandered around that basement all night trying to remember where the stairs were. They'd come up with a battered set of trousers and a checked shirt, and my soiled clothes were nowhere to be seen.

"Where'd you get these?" I asked Bert as I dressed.

"It's a hospital, Frank. There's plenty of extra clothes in the morgue."

I gave him a look of such strident disbelief that they both started laughing again. That snapped me out of it, and I found myself chuckling right along with them a few moments later.

"Really, Frank, one of the cleanup crew gave those to us. Where he got 'em, I dunno."

I was retying my shoes when a thought came to me. Ordinarily I wouldn't have done anything like this, but the circumstances were anything but ordinary. "Hey. Either of you have any idea why Jimmy didn't finish at law school?"

Charlie shrugged in answer, but Bert spoke right up. "Oh, that? He told me he was running a cheating ring. One of 'em ratted him out, but you know Jimmy—they couldn't prove anything. His rep was mud at that point anyway, so he agreed to leave school if they dropped it. He said his boss was gonna get him back in once things cooled off."

WALTER AND DEIDRE DALEY got there first. I'd phoned Walter after getting cleaned up, and he brought me an oversize pair of pants that was a big improvement over what I had on. The two medics had gone back out on duty by then, just after hearing an update which said Jimmy was not going to die. The bullet had not gone far, but it had done plenty of harm in its short trip, and Hanigan was still in surgery.

Bernie Kaplan appeared shortly after the Daleys, unshaven but sharp. He and Walter stepped aside to confer, probably discussing the potential legal fallout caused by our little foray to Thomas Pratt's house. Beth Ann, who had headed home from the party when I left with Jimmy, was now on the way back. I would have called Mandy, but I didn't know her number.

"That must have been a very tough time for you, Frank. Sitting there waiting for the ambulance." Deidre cooed, her hand on my arm. We were sitting in the waiting room, which was mercifully empty at that hour of the morning.

"The ambulance got there inside of five minutes, so it really wasn't that bad." I was having a hard time giving Deidre my full attention. The sight of Bernie and Walter talking was beginning to bother me. I couldn't tell if I was supposed to be over there helping, but I do know that I was worried Bernie might be selling Hanigan down the river, criticizing his decision to visit the Pratts even while the man was in surgery.

"It sounds like you did the right thing. Stopping the bleeding, I mean. He was lucky to have you with him."

That might have been just a poor choice of words, but it sounded almost as if Hanigan hadn't made it. I liked Deidre, but I was just starting to rise so I could walk over to Walter when an unexpected image appeared in front of me.

"How is he?" Bob Barstow asked, his face stamped in genuine concern. He looked as if he hadn't slept in days, which might have been possible given Jimmy's assessment of his go-it-alone investigative technique. His suit was rumpled, and his hat was in his hand.

"They said he isn't going to die. They're still working on him, but so far the word's been good." I stood up, amazed at how much better this small interaction made me feel.

"Hello, ma'am. Bob Barstow, Private Investigator. I've done some contract work for your husband from time to time." Bob extended his hand to Deidre, with a tone that was somewhere between basic politeness and hurried necessity. "Do you mind if I speak to Frank for a moment?"

I was a little surprised at that request, but it probably just meant he wanted to know why his client's husband had shot Jimmy Hanigan. Deidre offered to get me some coffee, and headed off toward Walter and Bernie. Although we were now alone, Barstow steered me off to a corner of the waiting room before speaking in a low voice.

"What happened?"

I told him, and he nodded as if receiving the one missing element to a puzzling equation. When I got to the point where Pratt denied killing his father, he looked me in the eye and asked, "Do you believe him?"

"Yes. No matter what else happened, I think he was telling the truth." I then quickly ran over the events leading up to the shooting, and Barstow asked another question.

"Do you think he meant to shoot Jimmy?"

"No. He looked awfully surprised, and dropped the gun right afterward."

"That won't make much difference to the police, but it does to me." He looked around, pausing on what could only have been the sight of Walter talking to Bernie. "You gotta understand what's going to happen here. Shooting Jimmy is exactly the kind of thing a guilty man would do, and the cops are going to run with that. That means I've been working for the family that's gonna get tagged with the old man's murder.

"And I'd bet my right arm that they didn't have anything to do with whatever killed that old man."

I had not yet considered the shooting's ramifications for the case, but now I saw the jeopardy in which Thomas Pratt had placed himself.

"You think he'll turn himself in?"

"Most guys in his position would, after talking to a lawyer. But I've spent a little time around his wife, and I'm guessing she won't let him put his head in the noose right away."

"Why's that?"

"She's convinced the old man killed himself. She

thinks that one of the others swiped the will from the safe, and that they're trying to pin it on Thomas."

"So who do you think took the will?"

"You know what I think." He gave Walter and Bernie another glance, and when he came back his face looked chipped from stone. "I think Belinda killed her husband after creating a nice alibi about not wanting his money. Then she got rid of the will so she could cry all the way to the bank. That's what I think."

"You got anything to back that up?" I asked this in all sincerity. I found Barstow's scenario pretty unlikely, but the whole investigation had swung back and forth enough times that I no longer knew what to think.

"One thing. But I can't share it right now. All I can say is, watch your back over at Daley & Associates now that Jimmy's on the sidelines."

This was too much for me, and I remembered why I didn't like Bob Barstow. His blind, brutish approach to investigations caused him to form conclusions long before they were warranted, and then it was nearly impossible to shake him off of them.

"Watch my back? For what?" I grabbed his arm with a good deal of pressure. "Tell me what you found out."

He placed his hand on mine, and I released my grip. "No. And you know why? Because you're a boy scout. You're not a bad guy, Cole, but you got no street smarts. I can read you like a book, everything you're thinking, and so can everybody else.

"Give yourself a chance here. Start looking at Belinda Pratt as a suspect instead of as a client. Then you'll see what I see."

He turned and left, and was long gone before I found the words to respond. I said them anyway.

"She's not the client. The dead guy's the client."

TWO POLICE OFFICERS had asked me some preliminary questions shortly after I'd arrived at the hospital, but it was nothing like I'd expected. They both knew Hanigan, and were more interested in where Thomas Pratt might have gone than in questioning me. Perhaps they saw Jimmy as the victim here, and perhaps they liked Hanigan enough not to ask the tough questions, but they did promise that a more detailed interview would take place later.

A tired-looking detective took my statement while Walter and Bernie sat on my right and left. The waiting room had gained a few customers by then, so we adjourned to a quiet table in the hospital cafeteria. I'd been up all night, and my energy levels were definitely dropping, but the whole scene still struck me as odd. The detective didn't appear interested in probing our reasons for being at the Pratt residence that late in the evening, and I quickly guessed that Walter Daley had exercised some of his considerable pull.

Not that I felt I had done anything wrong, in the eyes of the law or in the eyes of Daley & Associates. My bewilderment came from having so frequently warned Jimmy that he would one day get us both in deep trouble. I'd feared that day had finally arrived as soon as I saw the police, but apparently the detective didn't share in that belief.

At the very least I expected him to ask if Thomas

Pratt's lawyers had authorized us to visit their client, but he didn't bring it up. Walter hadn't mentioned it either, even when speaking with me alone, and I slowly deduced that the other side's lawyers might be withholding their protest. Their client had essentially kidnapped us at gunpoint, and then fled after shooting Jimmy. It was not beyond the realm of possibility that they were reevaluating the whole relationship, or might drop Pratt as a client altogether.

Walter and Bernie walked the detective out when we were done, and I sat there nursing a cup of coffee and wondering when we would hear more on Jimmy's condition. That thought reminded me that no one had called Mandy yet, which in turn reminded me that I still had Hanigan's cell phone. I'd put it in my pocket after calling the ambulance, and had transferred it with my other belongings as I changed clothes. I now wondered if Mandy's number might be in it somewhere.

I opened it up, and began scrolling through the contact numbers. I was mildly surprised to see Bob Barstow's name near the top of Hanigan's long list of contacts, but what I saw next truly astonished me. Just below it, listed merely as 'Belinda,' was Belinda Pratt's phone number.

Barstow's warning to watch my back began to bounce around inside my head, and I tried to fight it off. So what if Jimmy had Belinda's number where he could get to it quickly? He'd warned me to be careful with her, and had called ahead most of the time when I'd visited her. I even told myself that Hanigan probably entered the phone numbers for every contact in an ongoing case, but that didn't hold up. I didn't find a single number for the Grahams or Thomas Pratt.

My mind was fogging up with exhaustion, and I slowly closed the phone before putting it back in my pocket.

Someone managed to contact Mandy somehow, and she appeared just after I got back to the waiting room. I would have expected her to seek solace from either of the Daleys, and was truly surprised when she flung herself into my arms and began weeping on my shirt. I was trying to tell her that Hanigan was expected to pull through when Beth Ann arrived.

Tired as I was, and still trying to sort out the evening's events in my head, I might be forgiven for expecting Beth Ann to react poorly to the sight of her boyfriend embracing his partner's girlfriend. I needn't have worried, as my shirt front was apparently the place to be that morning. I ended up with an arm around each of them, neither one of them listening when I told them not to cry.

TEN

THE DOCTORS CAME BY a little after that to tell us Jimmy's surgery had gone well and that they were "very encouraged." He wasn't going to be allowed visitors until that evening, though, and so there was little left for us to do. Once the doctors had departed, Walter and Deidre suggested we go back to their place.

I wanted to stay at the hospital, to speak to Jimmy as soon as he came to. I wondered if he shared my impression of the accident, or if he believed that Pratt had actually meant to shoot him. Or both of us. I was pretty sure Pratt had been telling the truth when he denied killing his father, but that had been my feeling all along. Perhaps I was crossing Pratt off the list simply because I wanted to, and so I needed to compare notes with Jimmy.

"I think I'd like to be here when he wakes up." I said this quietly, surrounded as I was by earnest faces suggesting that going back to Walt and Deidre's was the thing to do.

Beth Ann had read my mind, and asked the others to give us a second to talk. They moved away with reluctance, but it doesn't take the Irish long to start talking about something else. Soon they were discussing the possibility that Beth Ann and I might be staying at their place for more than a day.

"He's probably going to be pretty out of it when he wakes up," Beth Ann whispered in my ear as we sat on two of the waiting room's plastic seats. "And what's he going to be able to tell you? He probably saw even less of what happened than you did."

This was a good point. As sketchy as my own memories of the night's events were, they were probably better than Hanigan's. Even so, I couldn't stop thinking about what Barstow had said about watching my back. He'd been staring at Walter and Bernie at the time, and I recalled that he'd arrived at the hospital just as I was preparing to challenge the two lawyers about their private discussion. I'd been concerned that Bernie might have been bad-mouthing Jimmy, but Barstow couldn't have been worried about that. He'd said he suspected Belinda Pratt of stealing the will and worse, but how did that translate into watching my back with my employer?

I needed to talk to Jimmy, and not just about the curious number stored in his cell phone. Despite the large number of people who had rallied around me, I was feeling awfully alone.

"I'll come back to the house once I've talked to Jimmy," I answered Beth Ann in a voice that was even lower than hers. "We were working this case pretty hard, and now I'm doing it alone. I need his help to keep this going."

Beth Ann rested her forehead against my ear for a

brief moment, and when I turned to her she was smiling like the model for the Mona Lisa. "You dope. You are not doing this alone. I've been with you every step of the way, and I know those photos better than either one of you. I already arranged for somebody to watch the shop for the next couple of days, and more if necessary. I'm with you on this. You're not alone."

And so that was how I ended up back at the Daleys' place, asleep in a real bed until early Sunday night, so exhausted that I didn't notice when Beth Ann crept into the room and pulled me into her arms like a child.

As IT TURNED OUT, I didn't get to compare notes about the shooting with Jimmy anyway. When he came to, he claimed to remember nothing from the incident. I suspected that he was faking this, but it satisfied the police and we were allowed to see him for a few minutes early that Sunday evening.

He was in the Intensive Care Unit, so he could only have a few visitors at a time. Mandy never left his side, so that left room for Walter, Deidre, Beth Ann and me. He was hooked up to some kind of seismographic monitor that beeped every few minutes, as well as an impressive array of IVs that had been described as antibiotics.

The earlier gloom had disappeared with the good news, and so it was a happy group that gathered around his elevated sickbed. He got the standard round of hugs and kisses from Deidre and Beth Ann, and some casual ribbing from Walter about being docked for missed work, and then his eyes fixed on mine.

Jimmy Hanigan was a man of many moods, and I thought I had seen most of them. Yet the best poet at the Beat, or the most fabulous car on the road, could not have elicited the look of wonder he gave me in that instant. He stuck out his hand, noted that it held a finger monitor, and impatiently swept the device away.

"And there's the man of the hour. Charlie and Bert came by just after I woke up. Said you saved my life." His voice was a dry croak, and I tried to take his hand gently because of his obviously weakened condition. His grip was surprisingly strong, though, and he pulled me in close. His whisper rasped in my ear, and his voice trembled for just a syllable or two. "I knew there was a reason I told Walter to hire you."

And that's why I forgot all the questions I thought I needed to ask, and just hugged him back.

THE NURSES SHOOED US all out just a few minutes later, and Beth Ann was ready with an answer when Deidre suggested we stay the night.

"We would, but Frank's car is at my place." She'd driven it home from the party the night before, and used her own car to get to the hospital. "And I do have to open the shop tomorrow."

Walter gave me a goodbye embrace, telling me to take the next day off, and suggesting I stay at Beth Ann's. Deidre was crying when we hugged, but she was the happiest weeping woman I'd ever seen. She thanked me several times in the course of that hug, and a moment later Beth Ann and I were rolling down the highway toward her place. I let a mile or so go by before I said anything.

"I think you're spending too much time around Hanigan."

"And why's that?" A smile played across her lips, and I saw it in the lights of an approaching car.

"Because you lied like a pro when you told Deidre about having to open up your shop tomorrow. Jimmy would be proud."

"So THAT'S ABOUT IT. That's where we stand," I finished, summing up the Pratt case for Beth Ann, who was sitting across from me at her kitchen table. It was nighttime, but we'd both had long naps during the day and there was work to do. "Exactly nowhere."

"Not exactly. A lot's happened since Pratt died, and you and Jimmy were in the middle of most of it. At the very least you figured out how the family functions." She took a sip of coffee. "Why don't we drop all the analysis and just go with this—who did you and Jimmy think did it? Were you suspicious of any of them?"

"That's its own problem. We jumped around a lot. We both crossed Thomas off the list when we first met him. He seemed to genuinely miss his father, and not to care about the new will. He said he believed his family would have been taken care of no matter how the money was cut up. His main disappointment was that his father wouldn't see his restaurant really come into its own. I think that was important to him.

"His wife was another case, though. She really didn't want to give us the camera with the party photos, and I think she was pretty mad that her husband even told us about them in the first place. Jimmy was afraid she'd get rid of the pictures, or download them and claim they'd been deleted. That's why we went over there un-announced…the first time."

"You'd think you would have learned something from that first trip," she answered with a smile.

"In a way, we did. Jimmy's antennae were twitching after Lindsay slammed the door on us, so he decided to watch her. We already knew Barstow was involved in this because we'd seen him outside Graham's office. So Jimmy followed Lindsay, and when she met up with Barstow he knew she'd hired him.

"We talked to Barstow a little later, and learned that Lindsay had him tailing Graham about a month before the party. It didn't seem likely that she'd hire a P.I. to sniff around the family if she were getting ready to do something illegal, so we reversed ourselves and crossed her off, too. And her husband still didn't seem the type to even think about something like this."

Beth Ann shook her head slowly, as if I were an amusing toddler. "You and Jimmy are such…*guys*. Don't you know that a mother worried about her kids' futures is likely to do just about anything? Her husband might have believed they'd be taken care of, but maybe she didn't. She hired Barstow to follow Graham, so it sounds like she wanted to get some dirt on the two people who were going to inherit the bulk of the family money."

"But she did that a month before Chester Pratt died, and rehired Barstow just after it happened. If I'd murdered someone, or stolen a dead man's will, the last thing I'd do is add another snoop into the mix."

"Maybe that's why she did it. You said that Jimmy and Walter both think Barstow's incompetent. Maybe she heard the same thing."

"They don't think he's incompetent. They think he jumps to the wrong conclusion sometimes." I was surprised to be standing up for the guy, but Barstow's recent actions had me questioning my opinion of him. He'd leveled with us about his employer, and was genuinely worried about Hanigan at the hospital. Even if he was wrong when he suggested I watch my back, at least he had seen fit to warn me. "They both say he's a good investigator, and Jimmy says he's practically an iron man when it comes to surveillance. Besides, how would Lindsay know Barstow's reputation?"

"Maybe she didn't. I'm just trying to approach this with a fresh set of eyes. Which brings me to something else. You and Jimmy assume that if one spouse is involved in the crime, that means the other one is, too. That might not be the case. It's one thing for a desperate daughter-in-law to kill Pratt, it's another thing entirely if it's his son.

"The same goes for Graham. His wife sounds like she really wants you to find out what happened to her father, but maybe she doesn't see that might lead to her husband. He hated Chester Pratt, he didn't want his wife to inherit her father's money, and he said he wasn't unhappy that the will was lost."

"But that also puts him in the same category as Lindsay. Those aren't the actions, or statements, of someone trying to avoid suspicion."

"Why wouldn't they need to be? He was only admitting to what you already knew. If he said he liked his father-in-law and hoped the will would be found, he'd have people contradicting him from all directions. The point is he had a reason to commit this crime, and his wife might not know he did it."

I turned that over in my head for a few moments, and was reminded of similar sessions with Jimmy and Walter. Like those earlier discussions, this one wasn't making the picture any clearer. I kept on getting the funny feeling that we'd come close to a breakthrough several times while hashing this back and forth, and yet the truth stayed maddeningly out of reach.

Beth Ann was reading my mind again. "I know this doesn't appear to be helping, Frank, but we have to consider Barstow's input, too. Right from the start he was telling you to suspect Belinda. She's the new wife, she was alone in the house with Pratt, and she gets half the estate no matter how much she says she doesn't want it."

She was alone in the house with Pratt. Those words reminded me of the time I'd spent talking to Belinda in her house, and finally revealed the thing I had forgotten to do. It was something I'd done in other cases, and I couldn't believe I'd neglected to do it here.

I had visited the Pratt house several times, inspected the study closely, and even sat at Chester's desk. But I'd never reconstructed the chain of events that would have had to occur there on the crucial evening. It didn't matter who the culprit was, even if it was Pratt himself. I should have considered each suspect in turn, and established what they would have had to do to commit this act. Then, combining that chain of events with the facts I'd gleaned from the interviews and the pictures, I might be able to start crossing people off.

"You just gave me an idea. We've been guessing about motives and what may or may not have happened at the party, but there's a lot we do know about the night Pratt died."

I stood up and began walking back and forth. "He had a habit of sitting up late, reading in his study, and so there was nothing strange about him doing that the night of the party. At some point he either succumbed to having been poisoned, or he downed the pills, shut his eyes and waited for the end. The sleeping pills make either case possible because the guy nodded off in that easy chair more often than not. If he got sleepy, he'd have felt perfectly safe in shutting his eyes down there.

"If he killed himself, staying down in the study guaranteed that Belinda wouldn't be in a position to intervene. But what if he *was* murdered? How could someone make sure he wouldn't be asleep next to his wife when he had the heart attack? He might have been out like a light, but she might have noticed he was in trouble in time to get help." I had a momentary vision of Charlie and Bert kicking the Pratts' front door open, and stifled the urge to laugh.

"I see where you're going, assuming this was a murder." Beth Ann's eyes focused somewhere on the wall behind me. "Maybe the killer thought about that, and made sure the dosage was so high that it wouldn't matter. But if the attempt failed…"

"A blood test would show what he'd been fed, and Pratt would be alive to say he didn't do it."

"If this was a murder, it's got to be tied to the will's disappearance." Beth Ann's expression grew less certain. "Right?"

"That part's been bothering me ever since Belinda and Kerry said they didn't believe Pratt killed himself. Even Jimmy thought it was possible that there were two unrelated events here: first we've got a suicide or a murder, and then maybe we've got somebody unconnected to either of those, somebody who saw a chance and took it. Took the will, I mean."

We both grew silent at that. Beth Ann exhaled through puckered lips before summing things up.

"We're absolutely nowhere."

THEY SAY A good night's sleep is frequently all you need to unlock a puzzle. Sometimes you obsess over a problem for so long that it becomes insurmountable—until the moment you stop thinking about it.

That didn't happen for me that night, but it happened for Beth Ann. We were eating breakfast the next morning, trying not to muddle each other's thoughts, when things came slightly into focus for my dear photography instructor.

"I just thought of something. You said you didn't think Lindsay would hire Barstow weeks before Pratt died if she was planning to do him in."

"Yes."

"I think we missed something there. If this was a murder, whoever did it had to have been getting things together in the weeks before the birthday. Barstow followed Graham for several days during that time. Of all the possible suspects, Graham's the only one whose activities we can pinpoint a few weeks before the party."

My mouth must have hung open, because Beth Ann tried very hard just then to suppress an expression brimming with pride. She was so adorable, sitting there trying not to show how pleased she was, that I stood up, walked over and kissed her.

"And right down the line we've been saying that Barstow collects great evidence, but always uses it to draw the wrong conclusion."

"Right!" she exclaimed, jumping up out of her chair. "He might have seen Graham doing something that has a *lot* to do with the missing will, but since it was weeks before the party, he might not have recognized it for what it was."

I embraced her then, and she hugged back even tighter. "Looks like we're going back to Tallahassee today, huh?"

ELEVEN

I GOT NO ANSWER when I tried to call Barstow on Jimmy's phone, so I headed for Belinda Pratt's house in the hope of finding him. Barstow believed Belinda had murdered Chester Pratt, and so I felt he was likely to show up there to conduct some kind of osmotic surveillance. I had no idea what he might glean from that, but then again I didn't agree with his belief that Belinda had murdered her husband, either.

I slowly rolled through the streets surrounding the Pratt house, looking for Barstow's car. He couldn't observe the place too well from anywhere but the street in front of it, but I wanted to make sure I didn't miss him. With the way things had been going, I was worried I would swing through the neighborhood right at the moment that he decided to go gas up.

This turned out to be a good precaution, because his car was parked under a tree three blocks from the house. I pulled in right behind it and walked up to find the iron man of surveillance completely asleep behind the wheel. I tapped on the window, and he came to in an instant.

"Cole. What are you doin' here?" Barstow asked once he had the window rolled down. He didn't seem annoyed, though, and so I tried to keep that going.

"Thought you'd like an update on Hanigan. He'll be

in the hospital a few days, but he's awake and they say he's gonna be fine."

"I already knew that. I dropped in on him this morning."

I looked up and down the quiet suburban street. "I've been thinking about the case since we last talked, and I have to admit what you said makes some sense."

"No, you don't. If you did, you'd be over at Daley & Associates. You'd be asking Walter why he didn't tell you he and Belinda once had themselves a fling."

So that was it. That was what he'd meant when he'd told me to watch my back. He'd been staring at Walter and Bernie at the time, and I'd thought he was simply curious about what they were discussing. But that was wrong. Somewhere in the darker corners of his mind, Barstow had become convinced that my boss had conspired to murder one of his clients.

With this new revelation it was hard to stay focused. I was after Barstow's records from the Graham surveillance, but his last comment piqued my curiosity. "Bob, what makes you think that Walter and Belinda were having an affair?"

"Pretty obvious, isn't it? They're both from the same town about twenty miles west of here. Same high school and everything. They go back a long way, but it's not something either one of them talks about much." I hadn't known about this connection, and felt my heart begin to beat just a tick or two faster.

"They're not the same age, Bob. They wouldn't have been in school at the same time." I tried to remember if Walter or Belinda had ever told me the origin of their acquaintance, but drew a blank. "They might have met right here in Tallahassee, for all we know."

"Living in Exile hasn't done a thing for you, has it, Cole? We're talking about a real small town. Everybody knows everybody else, no matter what age. And they all know who went to the big city, especially when they go there themselves looking for work. Walter landed that bank job for Belinda a couple decades ago, and I'm betting he had a thing with her on the side, as well."

I hadn't known Walter and Deidre long, but I considered them friends and felt my face growing hot. "Have you got anything to back that up? Couldn't it be that he just wanted to help somebody from his hometown find a job?"

"You see, this is what bugs me about you, Cole. You're not stupid, and I kind of admire the way you stick to a case, but you got no sense. Lindsay Pratt told me that Walter introduced Belinda to Chester.

"Don't you see what happened here? Pratt's wife died, and after a decent interval old buddy Walter introduced him to Belinda. At best, it was a way of unloading his old mistress on somebody with the bucks to take care of her. At worst…"

"You think Walter is part of a conspiracy to commit murder? Is that what you're saying?"

"You tell me. Pratt had dozens of lawyers over the years, and Walter wasn't one of 'em. But when he was getting remarried, who'd he see about a prenup and a will? Walter. Whose idea you think that was? The guy who'd never hired Daley & Associates before, or the gal Walter introduced him to?"

It was only midmorning, but I began to really feel the heat. My mind raced over the details of Barstow's accusations, and unfortunately it began to find evidence that supported his claim.

I'd simply assumed that Walter met Belinda through his friend Chester Pratt, and Walter had never told me anything different. I was a little surprised that no one in the Pratt family had mentioned this connection to me, but then I recalled Belinda's familiar way of referring to her dead husband's lawyer. Giving it some thought, I realized that she'd always referred to him as "Walter," never "Walter Daley," or "Chet's lawyer," or anything like that.

But there was more. When the toxicology results were about to be released, Jimmy had warned me to call the firm before going to see Belinda. He'd explained this as a considerate gesture to the grieving widow, but what if it was something else? Belinda had already known the results when I saw her that day, and I had never asked who had given her that information.

Now it seemed likely that Walter had made that notification himself. Was it such a stretch to imagine him coaching Belinda through her lines, preparing the witness before his hapless investigator showed up to ask prearranged questions? Was it even possible that I, the novice, had been dispatched to interview Belinda so many times because I was unlikely to figure out what was going on?

It didn't escape my attention that Jimmy Hanigan would have been part and parcel of this scheme—and the discovery of Belinda's number in his cell phone now took on a sinister coloring. On Saturday he'd known that Lindsay had called Belinda, threatening to tell the police her suspicions about Graham's fidelity. That was a dirty piece of family laundry, but Belinda had told Hanigan (or Walter) about it right away.

What had the paramedic said about Jimmy's dismissal from law school? That he'd run a cheating ring. And that Walter was smoothing the way for his return to higher education.

I even heard Walter's unguarded comment at the Daley house when Jimmy had protested Bernie's inclusion in the reenactment of the birthday party: *Ten years from now, you two will be the firm's best lawyers, and you'll be best friends, too.*

Walter, Bernie and Jimmy. And there was no Frank Cole anywhere on that list.

"Yeah." Barstow's head bobbed as if we were both appreciating the same song. "You're startin' to see it, aren't you? I told Jimmy the same thing this morning, just to watch his reaction. 'Course he denied it, but what else could he do?

"They're snowin' you, Cole. That's why they didn't tell you about Walter and Belinda."

BOB BARSTOW WAS probably right about one thing: he'd said anybody could tell what I was thinking just by looking at me. Perhaps that's true, but then again it didn't take a psychic to see I was steamed when I came through the reception area at Daley & Associates.

I wanted to speak to Walter, and so I did try to slip through without attracting attention, but that didn't fool anybody in the front office. They didn't try to stop me, but it was no accident that Emil Tabor stepped into the long hallway just as I was nearing its end.

He was walking quickly, and I could tell from the look on his face that someone up front had called him. He wore a navy blue suit and some kind of impressionist tie, but what I noticed most was that he was on a collision course with me.

"Hello, Frank. What's up?" he asked once we were within a few feet of each other, and he didn't divert from my path as the distance closed. Neither did I, so we both stopped just short of contact.

"I need to see Walter, Emil."

"I'm afraid Walter's just a little busy right now, Frank. Is this something I can help you with?" Emil's voice was natural and smooth, and left me wondering if he was in on the subterfuge involving Belinda Pratt.

"I don't think so, Emil. Whether he knows it or not, Walter needs to see me right away. It's important, and it's about the Pratt case."

"Why don't we take a walk out back, Frank? Get some air, talk this over. Maybe reconsider our words before we actually speak them where they can cause trouble. I always take a walk out there when I'm a little…energized."

"I don't want to go out back, Emil."

"It's not a request, Frank." I had never been on the receiving end of Emil's chief-of-staff routine, and the change was surprising. His face had dropped into a mask of disapproval, and his tone was flat. "You come outside with me and let me help you sort this out, or you go home until you've cooled off. No one sees Walter looking like you do."

Emil frequently reminded me of the office manager who'd run my business years before, and until that moment I'd felt the comparison arose only from the similarity in their jobs. I now saw that Emil Tabor guarded Walter Daley in much the same way that my office manager had protected me. She'd routinely stepped in front of a wide variety of pushy salesmen, irksome clients, and probably even a few hot-tempered software developers in my employ. The memory made me soften just a touch, and Emil instantly reverted to his normal manner.

"Come on, the air will do us both some good." He took my arm, and steered me down a side hallway toward a door that led to the picnic area. No one was out there at that time of day, and we walked across the grass in no particular direction. "I really do come out here when I need to clear my thoughts. It's a very peaceful setting, and you can get some real thinking done."

"I don't need to do any thinking just yet, Emil. I need some answers."

"So tell me about it. What's bothering you?"

The breeze shook the foliage in the trees overhead, and an invisible bird chirped intermittently somewhere up there. Despite my annoyance at being thwarted, I discovered I actually was calming down. At least enough to wonder if following one of Bob Barstow's deductive leaps into my boss's office might just be something to reconsider.

"I can't tell you what's bothering me."

"So tell me something that's not."

OF COURSE EMIL wheedled it out of me, sitting across one of the wooden picnic tables and nodding his head as if weighing the merits of what I'd told him. I was waiting for him to try to make some kind of excuse for Walter, so his response was not what I expected.

"For what it's worth, I told Walter to take you into his confidence when he assigned you and Jimmy to this thing, but he wouldn't listen. Your friend Barstow is wrong about any hanky-panky going on here, but it is true that Walter intentionally left you in the dark about his friendship with Belinda."

"Sorry, Emil, but that's not good enough. How do I know you're not just saying that?"

"Because I can prove it. You said Belinda would have inherited all of Pratt's money if she'd just kept quiet about the first will we drew up. That's correct, but at first she didn't know it existed. When she found out, she insisted on having it changed.

"It seems that Chester Pratt wasn't above lying to his lawyer, any more than he was above lying to his children or his wife. Walter suspected Belinda didn't know about the first will, but Pratt assured him that she was perfectly happy with it."

He cleared his throat uncomfortably, and leaned in a little closer. "Walter suggested that I find a way to intervene at that time. Professionally speaking, it would not have been right for Walter to ask Belinda her opinion of the will, particularly if our client had intentionally failed to tell her."

I let that sink in, seeing more and more of my old

office manager in the man seated across from me. "So you asked her."

"Give me credit for a little more finesse than that, Frank. I called the Pratt house to ask if our bill had been received, at a time when I knew Chester Pratt wasn't home. As you might expect, his wife asked what the bill was for and I accidentally spilled the beans."

"I bet Chester wasn't happy about that."

"He did see through the subterfuge, but it was too late by then. I hope this satisfies you that we were not in cahoots with Mrs. Pratt to steal her husband's millions. Far from it."

I breathed a sigh of relief. I hadn't wanted to believe Barstow's accusation, but Walter's ill-considered decision to hide his past association with Belinda had left me open to the suggestion. I still meant to take this up with him, but I now had a new question for Emil.

"You were a little more involved in the drafting of the new will than usual, weren't you?"

"I did meet the Pratts at the door, just to make certain that they were in a civil frame of mind."

"There was an empty Daley & Associates document folder found in Pratt's house after the new will disappeared. We've been trying to determine if it held the missing will, or if it was the old cover for the first one. Is there any way you'd know the answer to that?"

"Of course. I had the Pratts bring the old will with them when Mr. Pratt signed the new one. I transferred the old one out of the folder and put the new one in its place. They never had more than one folder."

"WHAT'S ON YOUR MIND, Frank?" Walter beamed at me from behind his desk. Emil had walked me to the inner sanctum, but he left just after that. I think he knew I still meant to have words with Walter, but had decided to let his boss answer for his ill-advised decision to leave me in the dark.

I didn't take my usual seat, instead standing in the center of the floor. "I spoke to Bob Barstow today, and he told me you introduced Chester Pratt to Belinda. Why didn't you tell me that?"

"The very same reason you're looking at me the way you are—because it sounds suspicious."

"Barstow got that information from Lindsay Pratt. I doubt it's much of a secret. So why keep it from me?"

"Frank, please have a seat. I'm not your enemy."

"I'd rather stand, thank you."

"Okay. You want it, you get it." The fatherly Walter Daley disappeared for that instant, and a much sterner character took his place. "Yes, the family knows I introduced them, but there was no need to go broadcasting that information. I was afraid you'd let it slip if you bumped into the wrong investigator, and it looks like I was right. It has no connection to the case, and so I decided not to tell you."

"No connection? If it's not important, why worry who finds out about it?"

"Frank, here's one of the first things they teach you in law school—don't make your opponents' objections for them." My lack of comprehension must have showed, because Walter paused as if reformulating his argument. "It's like this, there are some things you can say in court that are almost guaranteed to draw an objection. But if you catch the other team napping, you might be able to slip something into the record that should have been disallowed.

"But if you decide not to take that chance because it *might* get shot down, in essence you're making the objection for your opponents. I don't do that. I was concerned that if you knew about my connection to Belinda you'd let it slip to the wrong ears. Sure they could find this out from someone else, but I wanted to make them actually do the work. Never assume the other side's going to ask the right question."

Insulting as it was, it made some kind of sense. I made a mental note to ask my lawyer buddy Mark about this, and went on to the next big item.

"Barstow thinks you and Belinda were more than friends. He thinks you matched her up with Pratt to get rid of her."

Walter pulled the phone toward him just then, and hit only two of its buttons. I assumed he was calling one of the finance people to tell them to prepare my severance, but I was wrong. He'd switched it to speaker with the first button, and his wife's voice came on the line after two rings.

"Hello?"

"Hi, Dee, it's Walter. I've got you on speaker phone, and I'm sitting with Frank."

"Hello, Frank!"

Baffled as I was, I still managed to return the greeting.

"Hon, Frank heard a rumor that Belinda Pratt was

my mistress, and that I introduced her to Chet to un-
load her. What do you think of that?"

Deidre Daley sounded like someone on the verge of
uncontrollable laughter when she answered. "Frank,
this is Florida, not France. Husbands do not bring their
mistresses home to dinner here. Belinda's been to our
place dozens of times, most of it before she met Chet.
And for the record, it was my idea to introduce them."

Walter gave me a scornful look, but he needn't have
bothered. After all the times Deidre had commented on
what a cute couple Beth Ann and I made, I should have
guessed that she would have been behind any match-
making involving Walter. I didn't know how to respond,
so Walter took the opportunity to let his wife go.

"Looks like you answered Frank's question, hon. I'll
be home at the regular time."

As soon as she was gone, Walter pointed an open
hand at one of the chairs in front of his desk. "Now sit
down, for God's sake. You're my lead investigator until
Jimmy gets out of the hospital, and I've learned something very important. Something that lets Belinda off
the hook, too."

I sat down, not sure what Walter could have discovered that would accomplish such a thing.

"The police have been holding something back, as
they sometimes do, and here it is. The plastic baggy
from Chet's desk, the one that held the pills, was run
through a battery of sophisticated tests. It's not something they normally do, but they hoped to find something that would indicate this was either a suicide or a
homicide, and the bag seems to have done that."

"What? They found prints?"

"No. They found nothing. No prints, no hand oils, no sign that a human being had ever handled that bag. The police feel that the absence of prints suggests this was a murder."

"I'm not following you."

"Well think about it. If Chet put that bag in his desk after downing a few of the pills, why wouldn't his prints be on it?"

It's not what you see, it's what you don't. If Chester Pratt had indeed killed himself, why would he care if his prints were found on the pill bag? And how would he handle the bag without leaving some kind of mark on it? I suppose he could have been wearing gloves, but why would he do that? The prints would have been there if this had been a suicide, and so their absence said this was a murder. Premeditated, too.

"This also puts Belinda and Kerry in the clear, because they were so careful not to touch the thing when they found it. After all, no one would have been surprised to find Belinda's prints on the bag. The presumption would be that Chet had used a sandwich bag that Belinda had handled some time before then. You know—you go to grab one bag and three come out, so you stuff the other two back in the box.

"So even if Belinda did kill Chet, there would be no need for her to keep her prints off the bag. And she probably would have made sure she touched the thing when she found it in his desk, just in case she'd accidentally left a trace earlier. But she left it alone when Kerry told her to.

"Which also puts Kerry in the clear. If she'd been involved, she wouldn't have stopped Belinda from handling the bag when she found it. But she did, and then she called the police. Far as I'm concerned, you can stop looking at Belinda and Kerry as possible suspects."

He cleared his throat, and folded his hands on his desk.

"As nice as that is, we're now left with a pretty solid conclusion that our client was murdered. The absence of prints on that bag says someone other than Chester Pratt put it in his desk. That individual was wearing gloves, and trying so hard not to leave evidence behind that the bag itself indicates this was a murder."

"Walter?"

"Yes."

"If the cops were holding this back, how do you know about the results?"

"I asked for that special testing, and offered to pay for it, as well. That's another thing I didn't communicate to you earlier, I never believed for a moment that Chet Pratt killed himself."

TWELVE

IT HAD BEEN a long day, and so I was pleased to see Beth Ann's name when my cell phone rang. I began imagining a quiet dinner where we would try to sort through the latest developments, but I didn't get to do that for long.

"Frank, I'm in that bar you told me about—Clark's. The one that Graham's receptionist goes to."

The day had been full of surprises, but this topped them all. I now recalled Jimmy's suggestion that we use Beth Ann for undercover work in places like Clark's, and honestly wished I'd taken the time to tell her that was a bad idea.

Not that it would have mattered. She continued speaking in a low voice, and I could make out the general hubbub which I associated with my own inglorious sojourn in that establishment.

"You said she comes here with her pals a lot, so I thought I'd drop in and see what I could find out. She's here, but I haven't been able to talk to her yet. Graham's sitting next to her at the bar, and he's pounding down the drinks like there's no tomorrow."

"That sounds like a pretty good reason for you to get out of there. What made you decide to do this, anyway?"

"Listen, Graham's three sheets to the wind, and his

receptionist is trying to get him to slow down. That doesn't sound like the guy you described."

"It isn't. It may not even be him. How would you recognize Graham, anyway?"

"Because I've been reconstructing his photo for the last four days, Professor Einstein. That's why I'm here. I noticed something in one of the pictures today, and decided to try Jimmy's cover story." I felt the words cutting into me, but forced myself to listen. "You better get down here right away. Something's really bothering this guy, and you might want to be nearby if he gets liquored up enough to say what it is."

"Listen to me. This is not a game. If he's done what you think he's done, do you really want to be near him when he blows?"

"I thought that was the whole idea."

"Beth Ann, I was inches from Jimmy when he got shot. What do you think is going through my mind right now?"

"Frank, I'm in a public bar loaded with white-collar workers. I'm perfectly safe. Now I need you to come down here right away. I think this guy's going to let something slip, and it would help if a Daley law firm investigator heard it."

I could see the sense in that, just as I could see that I wasn't going to talk her out of the risk she was taking. I promised myself that I would punch Jimmy Hanigan as hard as I could as soon as he was out of the hospital.

"I'm on my way. Meet me outside."

"Not a chance, Mother Hen. I'm in a booth in the back. You come to me."

AN ODD CHANGE came over me on the way to Clark's. I jumped behind the wheel with every intention of going straight through the front door, grabbing Beth Ann and pulling her out of there no matter who recognized me. I'd done something equally rash the previous spring, and although that episode ended in some gunplay, everything had turned out fine.

Unfortunately, I had not been talking to my girl-friend on the phone before making that earlier impru-dent decision. Beth Ann's logic began to work on me as I raced toward Graham's neck of the city, and a desire to see what was transpiring at Clark's began to take hold of me. If I ran in there like a madman, I would not just anger my girlfriend—I might also stop Graham from revealing whatever was bugging him.

I still had no idea how Jimmy Hanigan had slipped into Clark's the time before, other than a vague sugges-tion that he had sneaked in through the back. I suppose I had a chance of sliding through the front door unob-served, given the scene which Graham was reportedly making, but I didn't want to risk it.

So I pulled into a large parking lot behind the ex-tended building that housed Clark's and several other businesses. I tried to identify which door was the back entrance to the bar while also dialing Beth Ann's cell phone.

"Frank? Where are you?" She didn't sound worried, and the sounds of the people around her suggested that Graham hadn't ruined the party just yet.

"I'm out back. Are you all right?" I got lucky at that instant, because the same burst of laughter that I heard over the phone also emanated from a nearby metal door. It stood slightly ajar at the top of a short flight of concrete steps, and I started up.

"Except for getting hit on by fat married guys, I'm just fine. Can you get inside without being noticed?"

This was no time for hesitation, so I pulled the door open and walked straight in. I found myself in a short hallway with gleaming white walls and a red tile floor, and judging from the smell I guessed I was near the kitchen. The clanging of cooking utensils came from a large door to my right, and a waiter appeared in front of me just as I was about to try to walk through. He had a tray of food on his shoulder, and I remembered that Clark's was also a restaurant. When he headed down the hall away from me, I followed him.

Some early diners were already seated, and I just walked right between the tables. I emerged near the railing, which had concealed me on my last trip to Clark's, and finally got my bearings.

I didn't need any help locating Graham. He was one of the tallest men at the bar, and he was quietly arguing with his receptionist. She had his upper arm in a grip, which wrinkled his jacket, and was speaking to him earnestly. Graham's face was flushed, and he looked like one unhappy guy.

A damp, wadded-up cocktail napkin sailed past my head just then, and I turned to see Beth Ann seated in a booth just off to my left. It was far enough from Graham for me to safely sit down, but there was a problem: she wasn't alone.

The same fat guy who had shown me the way to the lavatories on my first visit was seated across from her, and I'd have to say it was a toss-up between him and Graham as far as who was more intoxicated. He was leaning across the table at Beth Ann, and appeared to be showing her pictures from his wallet.

This posed a problem for me. I wanted to get over to Beth Ann right away, to shield her if Graham decided to imitate his brother-in-law at some point, and to find some cover so I wouldn't be recognized. If the wallet-wielding fat man decided to fight me for his seat (or my girlfriend) I wasn't likely to stay incognito long.

Beth Ann raised a palm in my direction before tipping her head toward her new friend. She gave me a forbearing smile, and I finally understood what she was telling me. *Stay put. He's harmless.*

People swirled all around me, and I was bumped enough times to know I was well hidden. The throng around me was so active, and so animated, that even a sober Neil Graham was unlikely to pick me out. I let myself slide out into the mass of humanity, and gradually moved along until I was leaning against the divider that formed the wall of Beth Ann's booth.

"Hi, there. Come here often?" I asked without looking at her.

"It's my new favorite place. I've been handed two phone numbers already. These financial types know how to party down." Beth Ann imitated Jimmy Hanigan, talking to me while watching Graham. The fat man across from her was having difficulty flipping one of his wallet photos, and paid no mind to either one of us.

"You're telling me. I got pinched twice just crossing the floor."

That got her attention, so she looked up. "When this

is all over, we're coming back here. I am *really* having a good time."

Looking down, I caught the exhilarated light in her eyes. I'd seen that expression before, when other friends had helped with my work, and I didn't welcome its presence.

"Enjoy it while it lasts."

"I'm not leaving."

"That's not what I meant. The party's about to end." I motioned toward the front door, and Beth Ann looked up to see Kerry Pratt-Graham standing there, surveying the crowd with a concerned look.

"Oh, not yet!" I don't know if that was exactly what Beth Ann said, but I think it's close. I didn't get a chance to respond, though, because Graham's receptionist saw Kerry and waved her over. It seemed likely she'd called her boss's wife when he'd started acting up.

Kerry was dressed in a pink business outfit consisting of a jacket and skirt and a bunch of soft white buttons, and she passed through the crowd like a spirit. She slid right up to Graham on his open side, and he turned to her with a start. I like to think I saw him mouth the words "I'm sorry," but perhaps I didn't.

At any rate, Kerry didn't say anything. She laid a hand against his cheek, and it was as if she'd removed his battery. He gave her a helpless, imploring look, and she nodded as if they were nearing the end of a long conversation. The blonde had already let go of his arm, and Kerry led Graham out by the hand.

It was quite a scene, and when they were gone Beth Ann was staring after them with her mouth slightly open. She looked beautiful, and I decided enough was enough. I leaned over to the fat man and whispered in his ear.

"You're in my chair."

I HADN'T EVEN settled in when I recognized yet another face in the crowd. Seated near the entrance to the dining area, and also in a booth, was the scowling countenance of Lindsay Pratt.

"Did you catch that, Frank? Have you ever seen anything—"

"I'm sorry to interrupt, but I need to tell you something. Lindsay Pratt is sitting three booths down."

"Can I look?"

"Why not? She's staring right at us."

Beth Ann turned and gave Lindsay a long gaze. Thomas Pratt's wife looked very unfriendly at the moment, and I briefly considered resurrecting my plan to drag Beth Ann out of there. Having already experienced the business end of a Pratt family handgun, I had no desire to find out if Lindsay might be packing. Crowd or no crowd, I was one of the reasons her husband was on the run. Beth Ann, however, didn't seem to see things that way.

"Thanks for sitting down and blowing my cover, Frank."

"Your undercover days were over anyway. I vote we walk to the door without looking back."

"You really think she's going to do something crazy with all these people around? Remember, she's the only parent her three kids have left."

"I don't know what you have in mind, but I say we leave right now or keep up the staring contest. We're not going over there."

There was a time when people listened to me. Many of my former employees said I was a good boss and that they liked working for me. I'd even faced down a man I believed to be a murderer a few months earlier, but for some reason I just couldn't get my girl to hear a word I said.

Beth Ann slid out of the booth, allowing me to see that she was wearing a beige business suit similar to the one Kerry had been sporting. The jacket buttoned in the front, but showed a surprising amount of cleavage. I remembered then that Beth Ann had been advised to pose as a desperate single mother fresh from a local job interview, and I told myself to question her later about her job-hunting history.

I followed her through the crowd, and in what seemed like an hour we had covered the twenty feet which separated us from Lindsay Pratt's booth. Thomas Pratt's wife was wearing a plain black dress, and both her hands rested on the table in front of her. A quick glance on the cushion beside her revealed a small handbag, and I resolved to dive straight across the table if she so much as looked at the thing.

"Hi, Mrs. Pratt. I'm Beth Ann Thibedault, I work with Frank." As if that weren't surreal enough, she then shook hands with Lindsay. For her part, Mrs. Pratt looked about as happy to see us as any mother of three confronted by the people she blames for her husband's absence.

"Hello, Miss Thibedault. What can I do for you?"

"You can let us help you."

"Let *you* help *me?* That's a good one." Though hostile, Lindsay's voice was even and controlled. "My husband is hiding from the law because of your idiot friends, and you want to help me. Why don't you get lost instead?"

"Mrs. Pratt, you're here for a reason, and so are we. I think that reason's name is Neil Graham." I knew Beth Ann was fast on her feet, but I'd never seen this side of her before. She was practically guessing here, but the bluff was a good one. "Why don't we sit down and compare notes? At the very least we might be able to figure out why Mr. Graham was so drunk just now.

"Besides, what have you got to lose?"

"I LOVE MY HUSBAND, and I'm not letting go here. The whole world's been out to destroy that man as long as I've known him, his rotten parents included. He's a great guy with a big heart, but for some reason people see someone like that and decide to wipe their feet on him.

"All he's ever wanted to do was make people happy." Lindsay Pratt teared up for the first time since I'd met her. "He's sure made me happy.

"But there's always somebody like Graham out there, isn't there? He thought it was funny that we couldn't make the first two restaurants go. Mr. Independent, thumbing his nose at the Pratt fortune and then looking down at us because we wanted Thomas's fair share.

"Well he better get used to seeing me watching him. He'll slip up sometime, and I'll be there. He slipped up once before, and I saw it. He'll do it again."

I take no credit for getting Lindsay Pratt to open up. That was all Beth Ann's work, and so I let her carry the ball while I kept an eye on Mrs. Pratt's hands.

"What did you see?"

"About a year and a half ago I met a friend for lunch on the other side of town. When we came out, I just happened to see Neil in the parking lot of a motel across the street. He was talking to a young woman, and he laid a good one on her just before they went their separate ways.

"I'd never liked Neil, or any of Thomas's relatives for that matter. If I had my way, we'd've moved somewhere else a long time ago, money or no money. So I decided to find out if I saw what I thought I saw. The motel desk clerk was only too happy to tell me all about the tall man and the young woman who'd checked in for a couple of hours and then checked out again."

"Did you get a record of that?" I asked, having handled a case where a crooked desk clerk had rented rooms under the table without ever officially logging the transactions.

"No. Neil paid cash, and gave a false name. 'Mr. and Mrs. Brown.' Great imagination, our Neil. The clerk had never seen him before, and he never saw him again, either, I've checked. I didn't have any photos, but I know what I saw. I kept that piece of information to myself until Thomas's father made the new will, the one where he basically cut out his own son. That's when I decided to hire Mr. Barstow to get the evidence I needed."

I decided not to contest her belief that a million dollars constituted being "cut out" of a will. I already knew that Barstow hadn't found anything incriminating on Graham, but I wanted to see if Mrs. Pratt would lie about it.

"Did he find anything?"

"No. It sounds like Neil cleaned up his act. That was probably about the time his perfect little wife was convincing dear old dad to leave her all his money."

"You really believe that?" Beth Ann asked in a sympathetic tone. Lindsay had been drinking sodas before we arrived, so I knew her diatribe wasn't alcohol talk.

"Of course. You'd have to have seen her around him. It was disgusting, the way she'd string him along. One moment she was the perfect daughter, helping her father with his charity work, and the next she wouldn't even return his calls. She kept him at arm's length when it suited her, but when he had that first heart attack…all of a sudden they were inseparable."

Her anger seemed to get the best of her just then, and she paused for a few moments. "She learned that act from her mother. Caroline played the same game, sugar and spice one day and an ice queen the next. I can't say I blame them—Chester was a conniving, manipulating bastard long before I came on the scene. I can't imagine what it must have been like growing up in that family.

"Poor Thomas was the only genuine human being in that entire house. Did you see the way Kerry put the leash on Neil just now? I swear she stayed up in Chicago those first few years just to get him good and trained before she brought him home. She didn't want old Chester getting his hooks into her marriage."

"Just one question, Mrs. Pratt." I was speaking in

almost a whisper now, because much of the crowd had left the bar by then. "If Kerry convinced her father to leave her the bulk of his estate, why would she or her husband destroy the will?"

That stumped her. She gave me a long look, and her lower lip disappeared inside her mouth for a moment. "I don't think they did. I think they took the thing, and that it's going to magically reappear when they think the time is right. Either that, or Belinda took it when she found Chester."

The honesty of those bold, illogical accusations told me that Lindsay believed Pratt had killed himself. Obsessed with the man's estate, she'd assumed that the other beneficiaries of the will had reacted to Pratt's sudden death the same way she would have—if she'd only had the chance.

"Mrs. Pratt, there's one thing that you might clear up for us here, regarding the disappearance of the will. When you received the phone call from the hospital saying Chester was dead, why did you drop your youngest off with his grandmother?"

She blinked several times staring right at me, and then spoke in a strained voice. "You're not really much of an investigator, are you, Mr. Cole? Do you know that my husband broke down and cried when his father had his first heart attack? And that his three children were right there? I was able to explain things to Margie and Chester, but that scene really bothered little Thomas. There was no way I was going to put him through that again.

"And no, we didn't go near Chet's house on the way to my mother's, or to the hospital."

Beth Ann stepped in and saved me just then. "Mrs. Pratt, did Bob Barstow give you a full report when he was following Graham around the first time?"

"Of course. That's how I knew he'd be here."

"Could we see that report?"

"Why? He didn't catch Neil doing anything."

"Maybe he didn't know what to look for."

She glanced at her watch, and then began sliding out of the booth. "Sure. Why not? I've got to go get my kids from my mom, but we can swing by my house first. Maybe you'll see something that Mr. Barstow didn't."

The three of us headed for the door, and I let the two women walk in front of me. To put the icing on the bizarre cake of my return trip to Clark's, the same bartender gave me a small wave from the counter. When we made eye contact, he tipped his head toward the two young women leading me out of the place.

"Much better," he mouthed at me silently, while giving me the thumbs-up.

BETH ANN HAD BROUGHT the photos and the enlargements with her when she drove up to Tallahassee, so we headed to Hanigan's apartment after collecting Barstow's report. I was tempted to ask Lindsay if I could ask her children a question or two, still needing to know just how the youngest had migrated from his high chair to his grandfather's side at the birthday party. However, the ambulance tracks were still fresh on their front lawn, and so I decided against it.

We had plenty to work on, anyway. Beth Ann wouldn't say what she'd discovered in the photos, preferring to show it to me, and in the meantime Barstow's report was surprisingly complete. Leafing through it in the car, I could see that he'd typed up a log detailing everywhere Graham had gone during the days he'd been under surveillance. It would take a while to get through it, and even longer to determine if it contained anything of significance.

We had quite a load of stuff to carry up to Hanigan's second-floor apartment, so we were both happy enough to get the door open. We stopped right there, though, because over a dozen colored envelopes were strewn on the apartment's brown carpet just inside the doorway. I guessed that Hanigan's admirers in the complex had learned of his injury, and had been slipping their condolences under the door.

"What's all this?" Beth Ann asked as she stepped over the pile, her hands filled with enlarged photos of the Pratt birthday party.

"Jimmy's a pretty popular guy in the complex. I think these are from his friends." I was hauling Barstow's report and a box containing smaller prints of Chester Pratt's last birthday celebration. I set them both on the circular dinner table near the unit's small kitchen, and then began scooping up the envelopes. Some of them still retained the scent of perfume, and I tidied them up into a large stack.

"Really?" Beth Ann had propped the larger photos on the sofa facing Jimmy's large television, and now stared at me with raised eyebrows. "Landed in bachelor paradise, did we?"

"Oh, come on, you've seen the way women react

to Jimmy. But he's taken." I had a sudden memory of an incident from the first few times that I had bunked down at Hanigan's. It was late at night, and someone had come knocking gently on the door. I'd been asleep on the sofa, and so I answered it.

I hadn't been prepared for what greeted me when I opened the door. It was very late (or early, I guess) and an attractive woman with brown hair tied up behind her head was just outside. She was wearing a sports bra and very tight running shorts, and had been looking down at a very shapely calf when I opened up.

"Jimmah," she'd cooed in a delicate Southern voice, still inspecting her leg. "Ah've managed to pull a teeny muscle in mah ca-alf, and I was hoping you'd—" She looked up just then, and if I startled her it didn't show. "Oh, excuse me, ah didn't know Mr. Hanigan had company stayin' ovah."

She'd placed a warm palm on my chest, and whispered, "Be a dee-ah and tell Mr. Hanigan that Julie dropped bah. He'll know who it is."

She was gone a moment later, and in the morning I'd wondered if I'd imagined it all. She'd been wearing perfume, and now I believed I detected that same scent as I put the envelopes on the mantelpiece over the fake fireplace.

The memory must have shown on my face, because Beth Ann stepped a little closer. "I'm not talking about Jimmy. Do these 'admirers' drop by from time to time?"

"Well, yes, but I think they look at me as a bit of a mood-killer. Three's a crowd, that sort of thing."

She let out a laugh just then, and began sorting

through the contents of the box on the dinner table. "You're too easy, Frank. Don't ever get on this topic with Mandy, unless you want to see Hanigan get beat up by a hundred-pound art student."

I almost responded to that, but then realized I was being allowed to back out of a dangerous conversation and took the hint. "So are you going to tell me what you saw in these things?"

"Oh, yes." She murmured with true relish, just as she found what she'd been looking for. She handed me a large print of the now-familiar candle-blowing scene, the one where Pratt had been surrounded by the male partygoers. "Something you said at the Daleys' place stuck in my head, and so I began going over that picture again."

"What did I say?"

"You said it was difficult to hold the three-year-old so that he could blow out the candles."

I remembered that comment, when I'd been playing the role of Neil Graham. "Yeah, but remember we did that a few times. Graham would only have had to do it once."

She gave me a winsome smile before taking my hand and moving me over to stand facing the sofa. She selected one of the poster-size shots, a blow-up of the photo I was holding. I'd scrutinized it closely myself many times, and wondered what I'd missed.

"Look at the little boy that Graham is holding. Doesn't look happy, does he?" I'd noticed that before, too, but had chalked it up to excitement. The tyke was obviously exercised about something, his head tilted back in what was probably quite a howl.

"Look what everybody else is doing in this picture." I looked again, only to see what I already knew: Pratt, Graham, the oldest Pratt son and Thomas Pratt Senior were all blowing mightily toward the cake. All but the youngest one.

"That's strange. They're all blowing out the candles, but he's not."

"Pretty big moment in a little kid's evening, don't you think? You'd think he'd be leaning forward, puckered up for all he's worth. But he isn't.

"I was thinking about something Jimmy told you, about looking for the thing that should be there, but isn't. That kid should be blowing out the candles, but he's yelling instead. Now look at how Graham is holding him."

Viewing that particular photo had always been a problem because of the way the lighting worked. The candles showed every detail of Chester Pratt from the table up, but things got murky right after that. The light reflected off of all five faces, but the darkness still held sway over much of their bodies.

"The coffee mug is on Graham's side, and you can't see it in this picture. That's okay—you shouldn't. But there's one thing you should see that you don't. That little kid is squirming around because he's not close enough to the cake to have a chance at blowing out the candles.

"Graham is holding him against his chest, when he should be holding him out, away from his body." Her finger traced the very clear image of Graham's left arm, holding the youngest Pratt child against him. "We can't see his right arm."

"Of course not. You can't see much of anything just beyond the light."

"That's my point. You said that holding the kid up was hard, and I remembered you were holding him with both arms. Graham's right arm should be visible if he's doing that, but it's not."

I now saw what she'd seen, the thing that wasn't there that should be. Graham should have been holding the child out, to get him in range of the candles, and to do that he should have been using both hands. The child was acting up because he wanted to be moved closer to the action, but Graham couldn't do that.

"He should have held him out. Like this," I said, extending my arms in front of me and slightly down, as if preparing to bounce-pass a basketball.

"Exactly. But he couldn't. His right hand isn't in the photo because he's doing something with it."

The cold reality of her accusation seeped in slowly.

"He used that child as cover. It got him right next to the old man, with the lights out, and with everybody looking at the candles.

"And somewhere in that time, maybe when the candles were blown out and the room was pitch dark, he put something in the coffee."

For the first time that day, Beth Ann showed the unease which had characterized much of my investigative work. There is a chill that I sometimes get when I figure out just what happened in a murder, and it is not a comfortable sensation. She stepped up next to me, wrapped her arms around my waist, and put her head against my chest. I slipped an arm around her, and we both stood there staring at the picture.

"I don't think I like this work you do."

WE PUT THE PHOTOS away for a while, and I made dinner for us. I'm a gifted boiler of water, and Hanigan's cupboard was well stocked with bachelor survival food, so we had spaghetti.

We didn't take the pictures out again once we were done eating, but I did sit down with Barstow's report. He had a spare writing style, so I went through it quickly. Hanigan was right about his fellow P.I.; Barstow knew his stuff. He'd started by establishing Graham's routine. Knowing Graham's normal activities bought him the extra minutes he would need if he decided to stay behind and check out any unusual stops his quarry might make.

Barstow was also right in telling Lindsay Pratt that he hadn't seen Graham doing anything suspicious in the days he'd been on the job. The tail revealed little more than Graham's long hours at work, his standard one-drink trip to Clark's two or three times a week, and normal household shopping.

That, more than anything else, is why his trip to Hardy's Rare Books caught my eye. Chester Pratt had been sitting up with a book of old maps the night he died, and I'd been told the book was a gift from his daughter. It made sense that the son-in-law who disliked him hadn't taken an interest in his birthday present, and I'd thought nothing of it until now.

Graham's connection to the book was practically mandatory if he was the killer. No matter how strong the overdose, it was important that Pratt be in the study when it happened. If he'd been upstairs, there was a chance that Belinda might keep him alive until help got there, or even that he might blurt out a final message that proved he hadn't poisoned himself.

The gift book had kept him in the study, so its origin now became highly significant.

Not conclusive, however. Even if the gift came from this rare book shop, it still could have been selected by Graham's wife. Graham might simply have been carrying out an errand for Kerry when he visited the store. Thinking it through, I decided that the people who worked there might be able to tell me if Kerry had been involved in the purchase. If she hadn't, it would mean that the man who openly despised Chester Pratt had gone gift-shopping for him over a month before his birthday party.

Of course Graham might have been there for a completely different reason, and the gift book might have come from somewhere else, but now I had something I could verify. One of the most galling things about this investigation had been the lack of leads that could be followed up, and facts that could be proved or disproved. Here was something I could really sink my teeth into.

I looked up from the report just then, and something in a photo on Hanigan's wall caught my eye. I'd seen the picture before, but now I thought I recognized one of the characters. The picture was only three by five, and it depicted a humorous scene in which Hanigan and three other twentysomethings were gathered around a kitchen table somewhere. They were wearing pointed hats covered in stars, and were obviously imitating wizards for some reason.

Hanigan stood in the center, his arms around the man and woman on either side of him. They were all enjoying a good laugh, and now I saw what had caught my eye. The man on Hanigan's right was the same guy who had loaned us his car the other day. His untamed thatch of brown hair stuck out from under the wizard hat, and he was looking at Hanigan with an expression that was akin to worship.

I studied the textbooks strewn across the kitchen table in the photo, and soon recognized a copy of Black's Law Dictionary. The picture must have been taken during Jimmy's abbreviated stay at law school, and the man who had loaned us his car seemed to have been one of his classmates. I didn't get to ponder this for long, however.

"Frank?" Beth Ann called quietly from the living room a few feet away. She'd propped the enlarged photographs on the sofa, and was sketching a rough diagram based on what she was seeing. It showed the locations of the partygoers from just before the dining-room lights were turned out to when they came back on.

"I've been staring at these things, trying to see when the Pratt kid left the high chair. He's on the other side of the table from Graham, so if Graham went and got him, it's even more support for the idea that he used the kid for cover.

"The problem is, there's no photo covering that time frame. The kid could have hopped down and walked around the table himself for all we know."

"I thought about asking Lindsay if we could talk to the kids when we were there tonight, maybe ask these questions, but I didn't want to push our luck. She'd agreed to give us Barstow's report, so I decided to let it go. Besides, I'm not sure if the kids would even remember something like that."

Beth Ann set the photo on the table with an air of decision. "You know, it might be better to leave them out of this after all. That picture really rattled me, when I realized he used the little boy for cover. Maybe it would be better if the kid doesn't know he was used to help poison his grandfather."

That hadn't occurred to me before, and it seemed to bother Beth Ann, so I steered the conversation away from it.

"So let's go ahead and drop it. We've got a picture that suggests Graham was hiding something when the candles were being blown out, so let's backtrack from there. What would it be, and how hard would it be to conceal?"

"He ended up with only one free hand, so it would have to be pretty small."

"A bunch of pills might not dissolve completely in a mug of coffee, so he'd probably ground them into powder."

"So he'd need a small container, a tube maybe, that

he could easily palm until the lights went out. Then, he'd need to be able to open it with one hand."

This kind of thinking always raises more questions than it answers, but those questions are absolute gold. You actually start to see the problems the suspect encountered, and those problems frequently reveal the killer's plan.

"He'd have to open it with one hand, and pour it in while holding a struggling child."

"And he might not have expected the kid to struggle. Maybe he spilled some of it."

Finally. Like the absence of fingerprints on the drug baggy, this was a line of reasoning that might yield a solid clue. Finding traces of that powder would greatly strengthen our investigation.

"We already know that all the dishes and utensils went into the washer that night, so any traces that they might have held are long gone. What about the tablecloth? Did it look like it was definitely going into the laundry?"

We both began searching the pictures for signs of spills, and there were plenty. That didn't necessarily mean the covering had gone into the laundry that night, but the odds were high that it had been washed sometime since then.

"What about the child?" Beth Ann asked, her voice getting low and quiet. I wondered if it might be time to stop the discussion, but she continued. "He was struggling with Graham, and he might have gotten some of the powder on him."

Little Thomas Pratt had worn a white sailor suit to

the party, one with a back flap that tied in the front like a neckerchief. The picture was too dark to be sure, but there didn't seem to be anything on his pant legs.

"Maybe we're asking too much of the pictures, Beth Ann. We can talk to Lindsay in the morning, ask her if she saw something on the kid's clothes that night when she undressed him for bed. That outfit's kinda special, too, so maybe it didn't get washed every time it was worn. If we get lucky, it might not have even gone into the wash yet."

Beth Ann's eyes had become slightly unfocused, so I knew she wasn't perusing the photos at that moment. Her mouth puckered ever so slightly, and I waited for whatever was bothering her to come out.

"I read an article once, an awful story about child abduction. There are people who cruise the malls, hoping to snatch a toddler when the mother or father isn't looking. The article said that the kidnappers would hustle the kid into the bathroom and change the outfit the child was wearing so that it wouldn't fit the description the parents would give to mall security.

"The kidnappers never knew how big or small the victim was going to be, but that didn't matter because the clothes didn't have to fit. But they couldn't guess what size shoes the kid would be wearing, so they almost always left the original pair on. The article said that parents taking young kids shopping should always know what color shoes they had on. That was the one thing the kidnappers couldn't prepare for—the size of those little feet."

She pointed at the small black dress shoe the youngest Pratt had been wearing when his uncle had been holding him up. It was kicked high in the air, about to swing back into what may very well have been an open container of poison.

"The shoes. They don't put the shoes in the washer."

THIRTEEN

NEEDLESS TO SAY, the chance that any poison residue had found its way onto that child's shoe was quite slim. Its presence there, weeks after the event, was something that just about any defense lawyer in the world could have shot down with relative ease.

But the possibility that an identifiable hint of that deadly concoction might still exist was all we really had. The absence of fingerprints on the drug baggy might indicate that this was a murder, but it didn't point at anyone. With the coffee mug and the tablecloth both machine-washed, there truly was not much in the way of evidence.

The picture of Graham, holding the struggling child with only one arm when he would have been best positioned to poison his father-in-law, suggested that he was doing something very wrong at the time. His purchase of the rare book which had kept Chester Pratt in the study, far from help, added to this circumstantial evidence when I confirmed it the next day. The shop-keeper remembered Graham, and insisted that he was the only one involved in the purchase of Chester Pratt's favorite birthday gift. His last birthday gift.

I found all of this compelling, and struggled for quite some time over whether or not to bring it to Walter. It was a legal question, after all, and the firm's lawyers probably should have been able to tell me if this case would stand up in court.

Except I already didn't need to ask them. I'd watched a different case collapse in front of my eyes the previous spring, and that one had included a coconspirator's confession. I knew that the case against Neil Graham, as it existed then, was not a winner.

That's why I decided to call Bob Barstow. He was still stuck on Belinda Pratt as his prime suspect, but when I told him what I'd learned at the bookstore he saw the possibility that he was wrong. He also saw that his earlier work tailing Graham might have actually pointed out the killer, and wanted to be in on the final act if I could pull it off.

That was why Barstow was seated on that same park bench across from Graham's office building when I emerged from the elevator on Graham's floor. I had a small walkie-talkie device in my suit jacket pocket, set on transmit, and I went to the hall window to look down at Barstow. We had walked around the block looking for Kerry Pratt-Graham's blue BMW and hadn't found it, so we were reasonably sure she was not in the office.

"I'm here," I said quietly, and he reached down and brought the day's paper up in front of him in response. That was the signal that he was hearing and recording my every word, and so I turned and headed down the hall. The tape would never make it into a courtroom, but I wanted someone to hear it if I did convince Graham to confess. I went through the doors, walked up to the blonde receptionist, and asked to see Mr. Graham.

"I'm sorry, Mr. Cole, but Mr. Graham isn't receiving any visitors from your firm. If you have any questions—"

"Actually I don't. I do have something I wanted to give to him, and I was hoping you might do that for me." I flashed her a pleasant smile, and extended my hand to show that the message was quite small. It was an expensive business card, printed on stock that looked like old parchment, and its raised lettering showed that it came from Hardy's Rare Books.

She looked uncertain for just a heartbeat, but then took the card and stood up. She told me to wait right where I was, and disappeared up the hallway.

She was back in under a minute, looking concerned. I imagine that her boss's antics the previous night had rattled her just a little, and his reaction to my message obviously hadn't helped. She stood there for a second or two, as if deciding whether or not to carry out whatever instructions she'd been given, and then took a deep breath.

"Mr. Graham will see you in his office, Mr. Cole."

She looked back at me twice during the short walk, but I was focusing on the entrance to Kerry's office. It was important that she not be there, and a quick turn of the head showed she wasn't at her desk. I stepped past the receptionist into Graham's office, and she vanished back up the hall.

Graham looked a little worse for wear from his overindulgence the night before, but the Rolex and the cuff links were right where they were supposed to be. A red Paisley tie stood out against a crisp white shirt, and a light gray suit jacket was hung over the back of his chair. He didn't stand up, and I didn't sit down.

"What does this mean?" he asked in a dry voice, holding up the card.

"It means it's time to reevaluate things." In deciding to visit Graham, I'd made the assumption that he was ready to crack. I was taking a big chance there, as his drunken display the night before could simply have been a reaction to stress. He'd been questioned by the police and accused of infidelity, all while his wife's brother was on the run. Even so, I felt I knew the real reason why he was so close to the edge.

"I'm afraid I don't know what you're talking about." Noting the lack of bravado in his voice, I decided to go ahead with my plan. It did not involve pushing of any kind.

"I don't think you wanted anyone to get accused of murder here. I think you tried very hard to make this look like a suicide, and not just to cover yourself. I think you never meant for Thomas to take the fall, and that it's eating you up."

His mouth came open, and his head swung from left to right just once, like a punch-drunk fighter. "Look, I don't know what makes you think—"

"Hold on." I said this in a low, even voice. For this to work, he had to see me as the voice of reason, someone who understood. "The police are closing in on the truth here. You need to limit the damage before they figure this out. You need to put yourself in a more sympathetic light. And you can do that.

"Everybody knows Chester Pratt fought you for your

wife's attention. You were afraid of losing your wife if she inherited all that money. That she'd spend so much time managing her father's charity that there'd be nothing left for you.

"That charity had already put a strain on your relationship, hadn't it? I mean, that's probably what made you have that little fling, right?"

Graham looked down at the desk just then, and I waited for him to say something. When he raised his eyes again, there was a look of fear in them that I recognized. It was the same look I'd seen in the bathroom mirror when the creditors were closing in on my business.

"I did not do it. I couldn't do something like that."

"All right." I stepped forward and sat in one of the chairs I'd occupied the previous week. "Take a look at this, then."

I reached into my jacket pocket and brought out one of the smaller photos Beth Ann had printed, the one showing Graham holding the Pratt child in the air. His face whitened, and the skin on his cheeks pulled back in revulsion.

"This is from the party, just about when I think Pratt was poisoned. I think the drugs went into his coffee, and that someone waited until the lights were off to do it.

"Look here." I pointed with a pen. "It's easier to see this when it's blown up to poster size—like they'd do in a courtroom—but you're holding the kid too far from the candles. That's why he's struggling. He's not close enough to blow them out because you're holding him with only one arm. You're holding him with one arm...because you needed to have the other one free."

I let that sink in, giving him time to guess that I had even more incriminating pictures in reserve. He was breathing quickly now, and his fingers were pressing into the desk blotter. I reminded myself to keep an eye on his hands, and resumed my original argument in the same low, reasonable voice.

"But you didn't want anybody to get in trouble for this. You know how I know that? The plastic bag from the desk, and the folder that held the will." He shut his eyes, as if in pain, and then forced them open again without meeting my gaze. "You were with your wife both times you came to the Pratt house, the night of the party and the next day. When you planted those drugs in the desk, you couldn't take the chance of carrying an actual prescription bottle. Your wife might have hugged you, or bumped into you, and felt the plastic. So it had to be a baggy.

"The folder was the same problem. Once you took the will from the safe, you could hide it on you because it was paper. But the folder was hard-backed, so you couldn't carry it out with you. So you did the next best thing, and tucked it into the bookcase instead of taking it.

"But it was the baggy that got me thinking. It was in the back of the center drawer, supposedly where Pratt put it after he swallowed a few of the pills. But if he was going to be found dead ten feet away the next morning, why would he stuff the baggy in the back of the drawer?"

He swallowed hard when I asked that, giving me the only answer I'd need.

"You put the bag in there because you didn't want anybody to get accused of murder, especially Belinda. She's Suspect Number One, with total access to the victim and a big payday if the will's not found. You needed to make it clear this was a suicide, and so you put the pills in the desk.

"But you were afraid Pratt might reach in there that night, weren't you? That he'd open the drawer looking for a pen or something, and see the bag. So you pushed it way back, too far to be seen normally, but where it would be found if someone searched the desk. The way they would if they went looking for the missing will."

He shook his head several times, his mouth partly open. "There could be a thousand explanations for anything you've said."

"Okay. Maybe I'm being a little too charitable here. You wanted to get rid of your father-in-law, but you also wanted his millions to go to someone other than your wife. If Belinda got convicted of killing Pratt, her part of the money would come back into play. You needed to make sure everybody was in the clear so they could take their fair share."

I'd stuck to my script until then, but now I was going to have to take a real chance. I was certain, from Graham's physical reactions, that he'd done it. I let an edge creep into my voice.

"Except it didn't work out that way, did it? The cops are almost certain Thomas killed his dad. The poor guy's gonna go to jail for murdering his own father. And who knows what happens then? Maybe his share of the estate's going to come to your wife anyway."

I pointed at the photo on the desk, my words picking up speed. "He's not the only one who's going to suffer here, either. Look at the picture again. Look at your nephew. You were holding him. Such a trusting little kid. Happy birthday, happy birthday, and all the while you were fumbling with the poison.

"How's that kid going to feel when he finds out that you used him for cover? You're wrong if you think it can't be proved. It was dark, and he was fighting you because he wasn't close enough to the candles. I bet some of that powder missed the cup completely, fell on the tablecloth, and maybe even got on the kid's clothes."

He squeezed his eyes shut again, but I didn't wait. I tapped the photo where the dress shoe hung in the air, and his eyes opened.

"Or on his shoes. Everything else went into some kind of washing machine. His clothes, the tablecloth, the dishes, the mug. And I bet you got rid of everything you were wearing that night, in case any got on you. But the boy's shoes went right back in the closet at home. No wash for them. And they're dress shoes, so I bet he hasn't touched them since then.

"I've asked the police to look at those shoes. And guess what happens if they find residue on them?" He didn't look up, so I answered it myself. "Sure, you can deny it. And there'll be a trial, with the photos and the lab reports and a little boy's shoes as Exhibit A.

"It's gonna be in all the papers. You used a three-year-old to help you murder his grandfather. What do you think his life is going to be like when he learns about that?"

Graham lifted his hands off the desk, extending them toward me ever so slightly, as if begging. It was an odd imitation of the way he should have been holding the child, had he used both hands and actually meant to help the boy blow out the candles.

"You don't know what it was like. You have no idea. We never should have left Chicago. Things were beautiful up there. We had our work, we had enough money, we had each other, and that mean old bastard was hundreds of miles away.

"But Kerry wanted to come home. She said her dad could get her a great job down here, that she'd hit a plateau in Chicago. I had no idea what I was agreeing to. I just wanted her to be happy.

"You can understand that, can't you?"

Now *there* was a moment. I'd heard confessions before, but had never extracted one by myself. I should have been pleased, no matter how gruesome the topic, but his last sentences had affected me in a way I had not seen coming. He stared at me, waiting.

"I can, Mr. Graham. I had rich in-laws myself, once. And I let them take my wife away from me." I had never uttered those words before. Or even thought them.

"I knew you could understand. I knew it." He sagged in the chair. "We came down here, everything was great at first, but then that mean old bastard began pulling Kerry away for longer and longer, and at all hours. She said she knew what he was doing and that she could handle him.

"I couldn't take it after a while. I started seeing this girl, someone I'd met at a convention. She was from out of state, but she'd come down here every now and then. She was more a shoulder to cry on than anything else, but I got scared that someone would find out. There was this motel desk jockey, he told me someone had been asking about me and the girl. I ended it right after that, but I was afraid that Chester knew.

"And then he went and changed the will. He was going to drop all that money on Kerry, money we didn't need, and I just couldn't take the idea that she'd start running with the real money crowd, people I'd never match up with.

"And if she ever found out I cheated…well, there was only one way to settle this, and I did it. I got rid of that son of a bitch, and I took his will, too. He was going to use that thing to ruin my marriage from the grave. I hope you believe me when I say I didn't enjoy a bit of this, Mr. Cole. Except for when I burned Chester Pratt's last will and testament. I can't tell you how much I enjoyed that."

THERE WAS A NOISE behind me, and the door swung open with a small creak. I turned to see Kerry Pratt-Graham standing there, wearing a dark blue business outfit and looking ready to commit a murder or two of her own.

"What did you do?" she hissed, her skin taut across her face and her eyes wide as she came into the office.

Graham stood up slowly, his hands out in front of him. "How long…how long were you out there?"

"You killed my father? Over *money?* I told you I'd

handle everything, that I was *always* going to handle everything! It was just a matter of time. All you had to do was wait. Why didn't you listen to me?" The words came out in a low, tearful murmur, and I was strangely reminded of the last time I'd seen Thomas Pratt.

I was just coming to my feet when she made up her mind to do something. She turned toward the door in one smooth motion, and took two purposeful strides which told me she was headed to her office across the hall. And not for a pencil.

"Please stay right here, ma'am." For the first time since I'd met him, I was overjoyed to see Bob Barstow. He moved into the doorway and placed one hand on the frame, blocking Kerry's path. Obviously he'd seen her arrive outside, and had followed her into the suite. "The police are on the way. We don't want this to get any worse than it already is."

LATER THAT DAY, after Graham had repeated his story to the authorities, I wound up in Jimmy Hanigan's hospital room. He'd been moved from intensive care, was hooked to only one IV bag, and looked a hundred percent improved.

"Look at you two. Best buddies," Hanigan observed from his bed, his eyes swinging from Bob Barstow and back to me.

"I wouldn't go that far." Barstow looked across at me from one of the tiny room's two chairs. "But I do appreciate your calling me like that, Cole. You could have left me watching Belinda Pratt while you brought this home yourself."

"Lucky thing I did. What size gun did the police find in Kerry's office?"

"That was a nine millimeter. Those Pratts don't kid around when it comes to iron. And from the look on her face when I stopped her, I'd say she was definitely gonna put a couple extra holes in her husband."

Hanigan grinned at me. "At least you had the sense to get some help before you confronted Graham." He turned to Barstow, taking on a slightly more somber look. "And thanks for watching my partner's back, Bob. I owe you one."

"If you can smooth things over between me and Walter, at least enough so he'll throw me some contract work from time to time, you can call it even."

Barstow plucked his hat off of the nearby windowsill and stood up. He shook hands with Jimmy, and then with me.

"Thank you, Cole. It helps that I was able to tell my client what happened, and that I was in on it at the end."

"You think Thomas Pratt will turn himself in now, since he's not on the hook for a murder?" I asked.

"You bet. Besides, the guy he shot says it was an accident." He gave Jimmy a conspiratorial glance.

"Don't look at me that way. It *was* an accident."

"Whatever you say, Hanigan. See you guys later."

The door closed behind him, and I resumed my seat. I still had a couple of questions for Jimmy, and wanted to get them out of the way before Beth Ann arrived.

"I'm proud of you, Frank. You brought this one home all by yourself."

"I had plenty of help."

"Walter wanted me to say he's sorry he didn't trust you more. Me, too, by the way."

"Maybe you shouldn't trust me."

His eyes narrowed, and he turned his head in a doubtful fashion. "What have you been up to there, bud?"

"Not much. It's just that I recognized someone in that photo on the wall at your place. You know, the one with the wizard hats."

"Ooh. My sordid past has been discovered." He didn't sound too embarrassed, no matter what the words might say. "I knew I shouldn't have borrowed Gary's car in front of you."

"He looks different in the picture, but once I figured out he was in law school with you I just had to look him up."

"Wouldn't have been hard, he was allowed to go back after only a year."

"Exactly. He's sorry he hasn't been by to see you yet, but he's got some tough exams coming up. He told me what happened."

"Now you know why I don't tell that story. No one would believe it."

"I did. Gary said you were kind of a guru for the people in that picture, that they were all flunking out until you righted the boat."

"That part's true. I had a good average, but I wasn't ever gonna make Law Review or anything high-powered like that. I felt sorry for the ones who were having so much trouble when I was skating by, so I organized them into a study group.

"It wasn't a secret, and one of the profs even said I was doing a heck of a job. But then I made an educated guess about what would be on a certain final, and it was dead on. I even had the group studying the exact case that was used as a question on the exam—and when we all aced it somebody got suspicious."

"That's why they couldn't prove you cheated."

"Exactly. But so many uptight academics were convinced I did that there was no way to clear my name. I got in touch with Walter, and he brokered a deal for the bunch of us. The rest of the group got basically a year's suspension, but I got a 'we'll see' status. Who knows? Maybe getting plugged while working a murder case will put me over the top and I can go back."

"Your story sounds familiar to me." I fixed him with a tight smile, and he was only able to contain himself for a few seconds. He burst out laughing, holding his wound with one hand while using the other to shake a finger at me.

"Okay, okay, you got me! I saw the similarity, Mr. Man in Exile. I asked Walter to hire you after you told us what happened with your business up north. I figured if I was cooling my heels waiting for some prissy hypocrites to forgive me, I should at least be working with somebody who could sympathize."

We both enjoyed a quiet laugh at that, but I still had one last question. "Jimmy, I have to ask you about that pop gun you were carrying."

"No, Bert hasn't brought it by yet. I think he's going to hang on to it until I'm discharged."

"That's not what I was going to ask. You were packing that thing in your boot all those weeks and I was never aware of it. Not even that time we got cornered by those bikers."

"Oh, I knew those guys weren't gonna hurt us."

"Maybe so. But when Pratt was weaving back and forth in front of us, you decided to pull the thing out."

"It seemed like a good idea at the time."

"But it wasn't. And I think you knew that. I think you startled him, and that's why you got shot." He gave a slight shrug with his eyebrows, so I continued, "I also think you could have talked him down without ever touching that pistol. So tell me this, if you'd been alone, would you have reached for your gun?"

He locked eyes with me, and spoke with a bland voice. "Not on your life."

BETH ANN CAME BY with Mandy just a few minutes later, and we all agreed to meet at The Beat once Jimmy was up and around again. Mandy was standing next to him, an arm across his shoulders, and so I took up the same pose with Beth Ann.

"I meant to tell you this before the ladies arrived, but I forgot," Jimmy began, slipping an arm around Mandy's waist and pulling her up against the bed frame. "I'm gonna be sidelined for a while, and Walter's going to need an investigator until I'm healed. He'll pay you what I was making, and of course I'll be able to help you from the office.

"So, waddya say there, slugger? Ready to take over as starting quarterback?"

The old Hanigan charm was working overtime, and

I will not deny that I felt a thrill at the job offer. That only lasted a moment, however, as Beth Ann pinched me in a way that the others didn't see. I looked down at her, and she gave me a smile that was nonetheless a reminder that neither of us had enjoyed learning the truth about the Pratt murder.

"It's been a long day, and we've got a drive ahead of us. We'll talk when I come back to visit you."

Hanigan tilted his head slightly to the side, and then briefly nodded like the king on his throne granting me my leave. I looked at Beth Ann again, and she answered my unspoken question.

"Yeah. Let's go home."

* * * * *

REQUEST YOUR FREE BOOKS!

2 FREE NOVELS
PLUS 2 FREE GIFTS!

MYSTERY WORLDWIDE LIBRARY®

Your Partner in Crime

YES! Please send me 2 FREE novels from the Worldwide Library® series and my 2 FREE gifts (gifts are worth about $10). After receiving them, if I don't wish to receive any more books, I can return the shipping statement marked "cancel." If I don't cancel, I will receive 4 brand-new novels every month and be billed just $5.24 per book in the U.S. or $6.24 per book in Canada. That's a saving of at least 34% off the cover price. It's quite a bargain! Shipping and handling is just 50¢ per book in the U.S. and 75¢ per book in Canada.* I understand that accepting the 2 free books and gifts places me under no obligation to buy anything. I can always return a shipment and cancel at any time. Even if I never buy another book, the two free books and gifts are mine to keep forever.

414/424 WDN FEJ3

Name	(PLEASE PRINT)

Address	Apt. #

City	State/Prov.	Zip/Postal Code

Signature (if under 18, a parent or guardian must sign)

Mail to the **Reader Service:**
IN U.S.A.: P.O. Box 1867, Buffalo, NY 14240-1867
IN CANADA: P.O. Box 609, Fort Erie, Ontario L2A 5X3

Not valid for current subscribers to the Worldwide Library series.

Want to try two free books from another line?
Call 1-800-873-8635 or visit www.ReaderService.com.

* Terms and prices subject to change without notice. Prices do not include applicable taxes. Sales tax applicable in N.Y. Canadian residents will be charged applicable taxes. Offer not valid in Quebec. This offer is limited to one order per household. All orders subject to credit approval. Credit or debit balances in a customer's account(s) may be offset by any other outstanding balance owed by or to the customer. Please allow 4 to 6 weeks for delivery. Offer available while quantities last.

Your Privacy—The Reader Service is committed to protecting your privacy. Our Privacy Policy is available online at www.ReaderService.com or upon request from the Reader Service.

We make a portion of our mailing list available to reputable third parties that offer products we believe may interest you. If you prefer that we not exchange your name with third parties, or if you wish to clarify or modify your communication preferences, please visit us at www.ReaderService.com/consumerschoice or write to us at Reader Service Preference Service, P.O. Box 9062, Buffalo, NY 14269. Include your complete name and address.